DIAMOND

GIRL

DIAMOND

GIRL

To Eli Winters –
Brenda Turner

BRENDA TURNER

TATE PUBLISHING
AND ENTERPRISES, LLC

Published by Tate Publishing & Enterprises, LLC
127 E. Trade Center Terrace | Mustang, Oklahoma 73064 USA
1.888.361.9473 | www.tatepublishing.com

Tate Publishing is committed to excellence in the publishing industry. The company reflects the philosophy established by the founders, based on Psalm 68:11,
"The Lord gave the word and great was the company of those who published it."

Book design copyright © 2015 by Tate Publishing, LLC. All rights reserved.
Cover design by Ivan Charlem Igot
Interior design by Mary Jean Archival

Published in the United States of America

ISBN: 978-1-63418-366-6
1. Fiction / Action & Adventure
2. Juvenile Fiction / Action & Adventure / General
15.07.24

Diamond Girl is dedicated to everyone who has felt the need to belong. Home is where your heart is, regardless of location.

Curtis, Summer, Trey, Jacqueline, Conner, and Venda, thank you for your continued support of my writing.

1

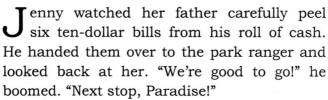

Jenny watched her father carefully peel six ten-dollar bills from his roll of cash. He handed them over to the park ranger and looked back at her. "We're good to go!" he boomed. "Next stop, Paradise!"

The dilapidated travel trailer bounced along behind the pickup truck as they moved farther into the woods. "This could be the answer for us," Dad said. "Not only will I have a paying job at the mill, we might get lucky and stumble across a diamond. Finders Keepers is the name of the game at Crater of Diamonds Park."

Jenny gave her father a grim nod. "Paradise" was another location in their nomadic way of life. It meant Jenny going to a new school and meeting yet another teacher. Dad was starting a new job in yet another small town. It only meant pure misery as far as she was concerned.

Her dad only seemed to care about the next adventure and didn't seem to understand how the way of life he'd chosen affected Jenny.

Small odds they'd ever find diamonds. The only treasure Jenny wished for was a real house that didn't have wheels and friends who took time to know that her middle name was Leigh and her favorite pizza was Canadian bacon.

The beat-up truck bounced along the black-topped road. "Here we go," said Dad as he turned into the RV parking area of the state park. "This looks like a good place to call home. We're not too far from the restrooms and showers. And according to the park map, the laundromat should be on the other side of that path."

Jenny looked at where she'd be living for at least the next few weeks from the smudged truck window. The forest was thick, and in this last week of September, the leaves on the trees were still green. She felt as gray inside as the sky above her. There were no other campers nearby. Now that schools were back in session and vacation season was over, they probably wouldn't meet many other campers except on the weekends.

Jenny's father had discovered long ago that it was cheap to rent a spot in campgrounds where they could use public restrooms and showers. He'd found the decrepit trailer for sale over in eastern Tennessee, and they'd lived in it ever since. Her dad had given Jenny the closet-sized back room to have as her own. He slept on a bed that they folded out after supper each night. First, they had to clear off the dishes and then lift up the table, which allowed the rest of the bed to be put in place. The RV was cramped, it smelled old, and Dad didn't do much to help with keeping things neat. Any straightening up was Jenny's responsibility.

"Yes, this will be a fine place to call home," said Dad. "We'll pull over here, next to these big pine trees. They will be a buffer as the autumn winds start to kick up." Jenny paid little attention to the trees as she scanned the area. She was more interested in their proximity to the restrooms and showers. The RV had a bathroom, but it looked like it belonged to one of the Munchkins in the Land of Oz.

"Jenny," Dad said as he parked and began unhitching the RV. "I'll take you to the school first thing in the morning and get you enrolled before I start my job at the mill. The school is a few blocks from the mill, so you'll be able to walk to where I'll park the truck to meet me every day after school."

Jenny's heart sank at the thought of a new school filled with children who belonged. She knew what to expect. The teacher would introduce her to the class and have everyone go around the room and say their names. Then the teacher would ask Jenny to tell a little bit about herself. That was a problem since her life was a total embarrassment. She never knew what to say. The truth was too painful: "I live in a run-down travel trailer with my dad, who can't keep a job. So we have to move around all the time. This is the thirteenth school I've gone to since kindergarten." There was *no* way Jenny would ever share her real story with strangers—especially strangers her own age. She'd had enough pitying looks from teachers and been shunned by so many children that she'd learned to be a loner.

"Sure, Dad, we can go tomorrow." As much as she hated going to a new school, it would be better than what they'd been doing the last three weeks. They'd spent that time driving around Arkansas with her dad knocking on the doors of any business that had a Help Wanted sign posted in a window.

—◈—

Next morning, after a bowl of Toasty O's, Jenny carefully combed her hair and tied it back with a rubber band. She looked in the warped mirror on the wall of her bedroom. With her shoulder-length brown hair pulled into a ponytail, her bangs looked pretty good. They weren't nearly as crooked as the last time Dad had trimmed them. They'd done their laundry at the campground laundromat. Her clothes, though found at Goodwill, were clean. She took a deep breath, scooped up her worn pink backpack, and got into the passenger side of the truck. Dad locked up the trailer, checking the door a second time as if someone would really think there might be something of value in the ugly tan-and-white vehicle.

"Come on now, I don't want to be late my first day on the job," said Dad as he jumped in. It took several tries to get the vehicle started, but finally it sputtered to life. As Dad turned to look over his shoulder and back out of their parking space, Jenny stared at the trailer, dreading what her day would bring. With a start, she realized someone was standing in the woods watching them leave.

"Dad! Do you see that?"

"What?" he asked as he turned around to look where Jenny was pointing. "I don't see anything."

"He was over there." Jenny pointed. "It looked like an old man with a beard standing back in the woods watching us back out."

Dad hit the brakes and peered again into the trees. Putting the car into gear, he said, "You must be imagining it. I looked around the area last night while setting up the RV, and I didn't see a sign of any other campers around." Dad could see the concern still etched on Jenny's face. "Really, Jenny, there isn't anything to worry about. I know these are thick woods, but you'll always be with me riding home from school. I think you're just imagining things. You do have an active imagination, you know!"

Jenny nodded but knew she had seen someone. That was the worst part of living in the RV and camping out. You never knew who your neighbors might be in a public area like that. Like Dad said, at least she'd always have him with her when they were out at the park.

They pulled out of the camping area onto the main road in the state park. "I'll drive by the mill, so you'll see where to walk after school. You have your key, right?"

Jenny nodded, lifting the silver chain up out of the neck of her shirt and showing Dad her pickup key. Most kids were called latchkey kids if they had to go home to an empty house. She was a pickup-key kid, always having to wait on Dad to finish his shift wherever he was working. She'd long ago learned how to do her homework in the front seat of the truck and how to curl up on the floorboards with the old fuzzy blue blanket around her to take a nap.

It took about ten minutes to get into town. "Here's the mill where I'll be working, Jenny," her dad said, pointing with his oil-stained finger. "As best as I can tell, you'll walk along this road for four blocks and then turn right here. See, there's the school."

Jenny looked at the school. The elementary school and high school were right by each other. That was typical of small towns.

Jenny could feel the butterflies in her stomach. Another new place, and of course her dad didn't think about how hard it was starting school on a Friday when there would be nothing for her to do. Everyone would be taking spelling tests and end-of-week quizzes, and Jenny would have to sit there and watch.

Dad pulled to a stop in front of the elementary school. "Home of the Rattlers" was written on the sign. "Look, Jen," he said. "Their mascot is a rattlesnake."

Jenny shuddered. "Daddy, does that mean there are lots of snakes around here?"

"Nah," he said. "I'm sure they picked that as their mascot because rattlesnakes are mean as the dickens, and they want to scare the teams they play."

Jenny followed Dad into the one-story building. The office was just to the right of the front door. On the left wall was a mural with a football player, a drummer, and a cheerleader. Above them, "Rattlers . . . The Tradition Starts Here" was written in red paint.

Her dad pushed open the beige metal door of the office. A large woman with bright blue eye shadow over her black-rimmed eyes sat behind the desk. The nameplate on her desk said she was Mrs. Miller.

"May I help you?" she drawled in a distinctively southern accent. It sounded more like "Maw I hep you?"

"My name's Jim Shoemaker. I need to enroll my daughter in school. She's in fifth grade," Dad paused. "We moved to town yesterday."

"Fifth grade, hmm. You'll be in Mrs. Lancaster's class," the woman said to Jenny. "Here." She handed Dad several forms. "You'll need to fill these out. You can both have a seat over there."

For what seemed like forever, Jenny waited on Dad to fill out the forms. As always, when it came time to put in emergency contact information, the space on the form was always left blank. They had no family. And since they lived like nomads, they had no friends to help out if there was an emergency. While Jenny waited, she looked around the cluttered office. There was a door with a sign that said "Principal" on it. The door was shut. Maybe the principal wasn't here today. Mrs. Miller had a jar of candy on her desk. She looked up and caught Jenny eyeing the candy.

"Here, sugar," she said. "Have a piece to put in your lunch." She then turned to Dad. "Did she bring her lunch? Or do you need to pay for cafeteria meals?"

Jim Shoemaker peeled off a worn twenty-dollar bill. "Will this cover her for a few days?"

"Oh, yes. That will last her a little while," Mrs. Miller said. "Do you want to walk with her to her new classroom?"

Jenny held her breath. The last thing she wanted was for her dad to walk her into her new classroom. The less she had to explain about him, the better. Dad looked down into his daughter's face. "No," he said, "she'll be fine. See you after school, Jenny." And with that, he was out the door and headed to the mill for work.

"This way, sweetie," said Mrs. Miller as she led Jenny down the wide corridor to the end of the hall. Essays and drawings done by students papered the walls. The sign above the door read "Lancaster's Place."

"Mrs. Lancaster?" Mrs. Miller knocked on the door. "You have a new student, Jenny Shoemaker."

The tall, thin teacher turned to the door. When she saw Jenny, her mouth broke into a huge toothy smile. "Welcome to our class! Boys, you've just been outnumbered!"

The boys in the class gave a collective groan, and the girls gave a cheer. "Shush, now. We don't want to frighten her off, children!" She stepped forward and held out her hand. "I'm Mrs. Lancaster, and these are your classmates. I have a place all ready for you." She saw Jenny's confused expression and said, "You see, we always have a new student desk set up, and we were starting to think that maybe no one new would be joining us. We're glad you're here, aren't we?"

The other students truly seemed happy to see Jenny. She'd never experienced anything like this welcome. Usually, teachers didn't want a new student, and she always felt left out.

"Kate, will you be Jenny's buddy? Help her with getting acquainted?"

A slender, brown-eyed girl answered, "Yes, Mrs. Lancaster, I'd be happy to help." Tilting her auburn curls in the direction of the desk, Kate led Jenny down the aisle. Before Jenny knew what had happened to her, she had her jacket on a hook, her raggedy backpack unloaded, and a stack of supplies on her desk. Kate helped her get settled in and finish writing her name on the new materials. "There," she said. "I think that will do for now. Plan on sitting next to me in the cafeteria."

Jenny gave a nod and sat back to give her attention to the class. Mrs. Lancaster continued with her lesson. Jenny found the right page number in the social studies book and followed along. It seemed as if she wasn't going to have to make up any stories about her life. What a relief!

Later that morning, Mrs. Lancaster approached Jenny's desk with a form. "Jenny, I just about forgot this! We're going on a field trip Monday to the Ka-Do-Ha Indian Village, and you'll need to bring this permission slip. Have your dad sign on this line. Go put this in your backpack right now, so you'll remember to get it signed this weekend."

Jenny did as she was told. What luck to be able to go on a field trip! Usually, she missed out on all the fun activities at the schools she had attended.

The day flew by. Kate stuck to Jenny like glue all day. It was the first time Jenny could remember that she'd actually enjoyed a day of school and felt like she had a friend. She could only hope that Kate would keep being her friend after the newness had worn off.

"See you on Monday!" called Kate as they headed down the concrete steps of the elementary school.

"See you then," answered Jenny with a wave. Looking ahead carefully, Jenny began her walk to Dad's job. He'd said four blocks before the turn. The last thing she wanted to do was get lost. Breathing deeply of the smells of early fall in the air, Jenny felt a small bubble of happiness float up inside of her. Somehow, this school felt different.

2

Four blocks and a right turn, and there was the sawmill. As she neared, Jenny's nose crinkled with the strong odor of freshly cut wood. There was a huge truck parked in the lot that had a load of logs stacked high, evidently waiting to unload them to be processed. Dad had told her he wouldn't be a driver on the timber lorry. His job would be planing the wood in the mill. Looking around the parking lot, she let out a sigh of relief to see the rickety old blue pickup truck, her home away from home. Unlocking the door and scooting into the passenger side, Jenny carefully locked the door behind her.

No one was around to notice a young girl sitting alone in a truck in the parking lot. Dad had parked at the edge of the lot, so the truck would get some shade from the trees that stood like sentinels around its edge. Setting her backpack on the floor, Jenny peeked under the driver's floor mat. Sure enough, Dad had left a couple of dollars there. Once they had time to get some groceries restocked after his first payday, he'd restock the snacks he typically left in the truck. At least for now he'd had a couple of dollars to spare, so she could get herself an afternoon snack.

She was hungry. It had been a long time since lunch in the cafeteria. Jenny carefully tucked the two dollars into her jeans pocket. Being careful to look both ways, she crossed the street to walk the five blocks back to Main Street.

Jenny remembered seeing a small grocery store driving into town that morning. As she neared the town square, she spotted it. There were jingle bells attached to the door. A round man with a shiny, bald head looked up as Jenny entered the store.

"Hi, there," he said. "Can I help you find something?"

Jenny gave a little shake of her head. "No thanks," she said, scanning the store, "I'll just get something from over there," pointing to what appeared to be the snack aisle.

The man appeared to go back to work on the crossword puzzle he had laying on the counter by the cash register. Feeling watched, Jenny looked up at the oval security mirror above the coolers. She met the eyes of the clerk and realized he was staring at her. Deciding not to linger, Jenny quickly selected a bag of potato chips. She set the chips on the counter, waiting to be rung up.

"You new around here?" asked the man, looking Jenny in the eye.

"Yes, sir," she replied politely. "We just moved here. My dad started a job at the saw mill." Jenny gestured back in the direction of the plant.

"The mill's a good place to work, been open a long time. My name's Lester Grimes, but you can call me Les." He gave Jenny her change, which she pocketed carefully. "You start school yet?"

Jenny nodded. "I started today. I'm in Mrs. Lancaster's fifth grade class."

Lester gave a nod. "My son, Tim, is in Mrs. Lancaster's fifth grade class. Did you meet him today?"

Jenny shrugged. "Probably, but there were so many kids that I don't know all of their names yet."

Mr. Grimes nodded, leaning his arm on top of the cash register, still looking her square in the eye. "Your mom working at the mill, too?"

Jenny was starting to feel uncomfortable. She'd made it all day at school without having to talk a lot about her home life, and now this man was grilling like a cheese sandwich!

"No, she's not working there." Jenny didn't elaborate on the fact that her mom was gone, especially since anything she said might travel back to class via Tim. "I've got to go. Thanks." With a jangle of the bells, Jenny left the store, leaving Mr. Grimes looking curiously out the window. After all, in a small town like Murfreesboro, you didn't get many new folks moving to town.

Back in the truck, she ate her snack and pulled out a math paper Mrs. Lancaster had asked her to complete. She'd been able to do most of the problems. Mrs. Lancaster had said the paper would help her understand Jenny's background in math.

Before she knew it, she heard a quick pound on the hood of the truck. It was her dad's way of greeting her. She gave him a smile as he got into the truck beside her. "So, how was your first day at school?" he asked.

"It was actually good," Jenny answered. "The teacher seems really nice! I have a permission form for you to sign for a field trip we're taking on Monday. I can't forget to have it with me, or I won't get to go!"

Dad looked over at Jenny. It pleased him to see her happy about something. "I'll sign it first thing. I'm glad you'll get to go." Even though he understood their way of life was often a disappointment to Jenny, he still wanted to do his best by her.

Within minutes, the truck was bouncing into the shaded canopy of the park. The air almost felt as green as the trees surrounding them. Jenny unloaded the frayed pink backpack and waited while her father unlocked the door. "Looks like everything's okay," he remarked as he opened the door to the RV. Jenny peered out into the woods, but everything seemed to be quiet with the exception of a couple of squirrels chasing each other through the tall branches.

Before long, her dad had dinner started in the iron skillet. "Thought I'd cook up some of these hot dogs, and you can make some macaroni and cheese to go with it." The water on the two burner stove was just starting to boil. "We'll go get loaded up on some groceries next Friday after you get out of school. I get paid that day."

That meant there'd be a week of random meals, thought Jenny. At least she would have the hot meals to look forward to in the school cafeteria. Even though she hated how they lived traveling from place to place, she was thankful to have food to eat, whether it was her favorite or not.

After dinner, they cleared the table. While Jenny washed the two plates, forks, and pans, Dad built a small campfire and set the fold-out camp chairs in front of the RV. It was a habit they'd started when they first began living in the RV. When the weather was good, they'd sit outside and talk rather than stay cooped up in the trailer.

"Hey, go get that permission slip you were talking about," he said. "I don't want to forget to sign it."

Jenny went inside to get it and also brought out the brochure Mrs. Lancaster had given her about Ka-Do-Ha Village. The campfire was turning into glowing embers as Dad read the brochure. She waited quietly while he signed the form and looked over the brochure.

"Hmm. Ka-Do-Ha sounds like an interesting place," he said. "And it looks like you'll even get to search for diamonds while you are there! Pretty crazy, huh, that there are diamonds in Arkansas?"

Jenny nodded, agreeing with him. "I know, I thought you only found them in Africa! Thanks, Dad, I'll put it in my backpack right now." She went inside, and when she came back out, she had a book in her hand. "I'm going to head to bed and read if that's okay."

"What book do you have there, Jenny?"

"Mrs. Lancaster has a big classroom library where we can sign out books one at a time. This is one from her mystery book tub. You know how I like reading those!"

Dad smiled. "You sure do, honey. Well, have sweet dreams, and don't stay up too late reading even though tomorrow is Saturday."

Jenny headed to the back of the trailer to her doll-sized room. As she lay on her bed, she contemplated her day. It had certainly been full of surprises. To her, the best surprise was the reception she'd gotten at the school. She never dreamed that she could be welcomed to a new place. As she drifted off to sleep, Jenny thought, *If only the kids will stay nice.*

3

"Let's hustle, class! We need to get loaded on the buses." Mrs. Lancaster was a tornado of activity. The students started grabbing their sack lunches and lining up at the door of the classroom. "Ka-Do-Ha Village, here we come!" she said as she led the students out the door to the waiting bus.

Kate was in line behind Jenny. "Sit with me on the bus," she said as they filed out the door. Jenny gave her a grateful grin, thankful she wouldn't have to sit alone or with one of the boys.

Once on the bus, Jenny leaned over to Kate. "So, is Ka-Do-Ha Village fun?"

"Guess you'd call it fun—at least we're not in class! Plus, it's always fun to search in the buckets for diamonds. There are ruins there from an early Indian tribe. They were called

Mound Builders. Supposedly the mounds and ruins that are out there are at least a thousand years old."

Jenny nodded. As they drove, it first appeared they were just going out on a street in town to the country. But once they passed an abandoned horse farm, they arrived at the village. The rest of the short ride to Ka-Do-Ha was uneventful with the exception of Tim Grimes doing his best to annoy anyone seated near him. Jenny may not have known who he was last Friday, but she certainly knew him now!

The museum and visitor center was in a one-story building. The usual commotion of unloading a class of fifth graders and getting lunches stored in the covered area finally settled down, and the students listened carefully to what the tour guide, Melinda, had to say. "The skeletal remains you are going to see in the mounds are replicas. There were actual skeletons discovered here, but they have been archived to a museum."

Melinda pushed her wire-rimmed glasses up higher on her nose. "Treat the gravesites with respect and read the display signs carefully in the museum. After you've had a chance to tour the burial mounds and museum, we'll go out to the discovery shed where each of you will receive a bucket of soil to sift and search for diamonds."

Mrs. Lancaster gave some final instructions, and then the students were off to explore.

"Come over here," said Kate as she pulled Jenny by the arm. "I've been here before with my grandma, and the mound over there is the most interesting. It's where the chiefs of the tribe were buried. That's why it has a cover."

The girls explored the mounds as the September sun beat down on them. Jenny had the heebie-jeebies looking in the gravesites. "I'm sorry, Kate, but I think it's weird looking at these burial places."

Kate nodded. "I know! Let's go to the discovery shed and look for diamonds instead." The girls arrived at the shed in time to hear Melinda give instructions. "Now these buckets contain soil from the Crater of Diamonds Park. You each will have your own work station over here." Melinda pointed to the worn wooden work tables. "We recommend you sift the soil through the first screen with the larger openings into the second screen with the tinier openings. Once you have the soil and smaller rocks on the second screen, carefully pour water over the smaller rocks to help you sort through them and to remove the dirt. Real diamonds often have an oily film on them, so the dirt particles won't necessarily stick to it. If you think you found anything that might be a real gemstone, call me over, and I'll check it out for you!"

It didn't take long for the students in Mrs. Lancaster's class to jump right into sifting and sorting the soil. "This is fun," Jenny giggled, her hands covered in the grainy soil. "Even if we don't find a diamond!"

Kate grinned back. "I agree. Like I said, I've been here before with my grandma. They say you find a diamond in every bucket, but they must be microscopic. I've never really found anything worth much."

"Hey!" called Zack, one of the boys in the class. "I think I've got something!"

There was a collective groan as Melinda went over to inspect Zack's find. She looked at it carefully, pulling a small magnifying glass out of her khaki cargo shorts.

"You know, you might have found something here," she said, peering carefully through her glasses. "Let me take it inside to look at under my larger scope. You can come with me if you want."

Melinda and Zack left, and the rest of the students returned to their search with renewed zest. They would be leaving after having their lunch at the picnic grounds, and their time to search before boarding the bus was starting to run out.

Jenny began sorting through her rocks with an intensity that surprised Kate. "Hey, slow down," she advised, "or you won't find anything."

Jenny looked up at her new friend. "Huh?"

"Slow down! You have to be more careful if you really want to find something valuable. Watch."

Kate moved over to Jenny's bucket and very carefully poured the water over a small section of the lamproite soil. She then carefully rubbed the soil back and forth over the screen's opening, getting the dirt off some stones. "See? You have to go slow or you'll miss a cool stone or diamond. Look at this!"

Kate held up a small rock, barely larger than a mustard seed. "This," she said slowly, carefully holding the rock up to the light, "this may be one."

"Here, let me see!" Jenny reached for it.

"Don't drop it," warned Kate.

Jenny carefully studied the stone. It was smooth and a golden brown color. "You really think this might be one?"

"Take it over to Melinda, and let her see it," advised Kate.

Handling the stone carefully, making sure she didn't drop it, Jenny walked over to where Melinda had returned. She was standing at the end of the tables. Melinda smiled as Jenny approached. "Think you found something?" she asked.

Jenny gave a tentative smile and handed the rock to Melinda. "Hmmm, this does look promising," she said as she looked at it through her magnifying glass. "Let me take it inside and see it through the microscope." She saw Jenny's concerned look. "Want to come with me?"

Jenny nodded and asked, "Can my friend come, too?"

"Sure," Melinda answered.

The girls told Mrs. Lancaster they were going inside to check Jenny's find. "Hey, no fair if the new girl finds something and I don't!" yelled Zack.

"Zack, that is uncalled for." Mrs. Lancaster frowned. "It is just as fair for Jenny to find a diamond here today as any one of you. Keep looking instead of complaining. Even though your stone turned out to not be a diamond, you may still find one in your bucket!"

Inside the museum, it was cool and the light was dim. It was hard for Jenny's and Kate's eyes to adjust to the change in light. "Over here, girls. This is where I keep my microscope for checking the stones."

The girls filed behind Melinda and watched as she carefully put the stone on the glass underneath the microscope's light. She put her eye up to the lens and carefully studied the minuscule rock for what seemed like hours instead of a couple of minutes.

After a long pause, she looked up at Jenny and Kate. "You found one, Jenny! This is a brown diamond, and I'd put it right at eight points. One carat is equal to one hundred points. If you were to have it professionally cut, it would be even smaller. Probably the best thing to do is let me put it in one of our keepsake cards, so you don't lose it. It really isn't a diamond that would be valuable for you to resell, but you can certainly be proud that you found one."

Jenny's eye's shone; she was so thrilled. She'd never found anything of value like this, and to have a real diamond that was her very own was exciting. "Let's go tell Mrs. Lancaster!" she said, grabbing Kate by her hand.

The two girls ran back outside jumping up and down. "Jenny found a diamond!" cried Kate. "She really did!"

The rest of the day passed in a blur. Back at school, Jenny carefully put the card with the diamond mounted on it into her backpack. She couldn't wait to show her dad.

"Congratulations, again, Jenny." Mrs. Lancaster smiled as Jenny headed out the door. "I'm glad you were able to find something. It was quite the lucky day for our class!"

Eight of the other students had also found small stones: six of them were small diamonds similar in size and color to Jenny's. The other two had found actual quartz. Everyone had been excited about his or her discoveries, but Jenny was thrilled. Sure, it wasn't something that was worth a lot of money, but it was *hers*.

Jenny's mind was racing in a million different directions as she walked the few blocks to the mill. It was almost surreal how everything could be the same on the outside and yet she could feel so special and different on the inside.

Using her key, she let herself into the pickup truck. Dad had left her a peanut butter sandwich and a thermos of water. No trip to the store today. It was obvious there would be slim pickings for food until payday on Friday. That was no longer a problem as far as Jenny was concerned. She felt rich!

4

Kate's grandma opened the door of her small bungalow style home. Smiling warmly, she motioned for the girls to come on in. "I have some warm chocolate chip cookies on a plate in the kitchen and more in the oven," she announced. Kate turned to give Jenny a grin and led the way on into the bright kitchen. Then remembering her manners, she whirled around.

"I'm sorry, Grandma, I forgot to introduce you. This is my friend, Jenny Shoemaker. She and her dad moved here last week, and he is working at the mill."

"Glad to meet you, Jenny," said Grandma. "You can call me Grandma Jo."

"Nice to meet you." Jenny wasn't sure what to do but reached out her right hand to shake Grandma's. As she started to follow Kate into the kitchen, she told Grandma Jo, "Thanks for inviting me over and making us cookies."

Kate was already at the white cabinets pulling out two glasses with cherries painted on the side. She pulled out a chair from the aged white table and gestured for Jenny to have a seat. "Milk okay?" she asked as she pulled on the silver handle of the refrigerator.

Jenny gave a nod and then turned her attention to the platter of warm cookies in the center of the table. Kate poured the milk. "Go ahead," she said to Jenny. "There are plenty, so help yourself." Kate sat down across from Jenny and set the glasses of milk on the table. The icy chill of the milk was already frosting the glasses.

"Mind if I join you?" Grandma Jo asked as she poured a cup of coffee from the percolator that sat on the counter. Her short salt-and-pepper hair framed her face. Sparkling, blue eyes looked out from her glasses.

"These are amazing!" Jenny exclaimed as soon as she could take a quick drink of her milk.

"Thanks," replied Grandma, selecting a cookie off the platter. "They're my secret recipe." She gave the cookie a little dunk into her coffee cup. Grandma looked at the girls. "So what are you two up to today?"

Kate and Jenny shrugged.

"Not much," said Kate. "We need to study the mineral list that Mrs. Lancaster is going to quiz us on tomorrow. But other than that, we don't have any homework."

"Mineral list? Let me see it." Grandma Jo looked it over. "Oh, this shouldn't be too hard. My goodness, I remember having to learn this when I was in school! Let me hear you say the list while you are eating the cookies. Kate, you go first."

Kate said, "I'll start with the softest mineral and work to diamonds, the hardest. Talc, gypsum, calcite, fluorite, apa . . . I can never remember that word!"

"A-pa-tite," said Grandma Jo. "You can remember it like you have an appetite for cookies, only you have to pretend you are a bad speller!"

Kate grinned. "Apatite," and she continued with the list, "orthoclase, quartz, topaz, the other hard one, corundum, then diamond."

Jenny looked at the two of them. "I don't think I can do that well yet. Let me look over the list a little longer."

Grandma Jo smiled at Jenny. "Here's how I learned to memorize the mineral list when I was a fifth grader. It's silly, but here it is. Tall Giants Can Find An Orange Quacking Tiny Colorful Duck . . . talc, gypsum, calcite, fluorite, apatite, orthoclase, quartz, topaz, corundum, diamond. Paint a picture in your mind of huge giants searching for tiny orange quacking ducks, and you'll never forget it."

Jenny smiled back at Grandma Jo and repeated, "Tall Giants Can Find An Orange Quacking Tiny Colorful Duck."

"You might not know all of the scientific terms quite yet, but if you remember that acrostic and partner it with the actual mineral names, I'll bet you'll make a one hundred on that quiz tomorrow."

Jenny nodded, a little bit in wonder. Kate had told her on the bus ride back from the field trip how she had to live with her grandmother since her parents had been killed in a car crash, but Jenny had pictured an old white-haired woman sitting in a rocker on the porch. Kate's grandma seemed young, and she was certainly energetic. *She's also a wonderful cook and teacher!* Jenny thought as she reached for another cookie.

"So, Jenny, how long have you lived here in Murfreesboro?" asked Grandma Jo.

Jenny looked up with a little start. The children at school and Mrs. Lancaster had been so accepting she'd sort of let down the wall of worry that someone would ask about her past. Now, here was Kate's grandma asking her questions like Lester Grimes.

Jenny swallowed her bite of cookie slowly. "We moved here last week."

"Really? I haven't seen you in town. Where do you all live? Did you rent the Garrison place? I know they had it cleaned up and ready for someone to move in."

Jenny hesitated. She'd made it this far not revealing that she lived out at the state park. Kate really hadn't pushed her to tell where she lived. It was almost as if Kate could sense that Jenny didn't want to share that information, and so she hadn't pried. Jenny looked over at Kate, who was more interested in selecting her next cookie than in Jenny's answer. "My dad and I live in the Crater of Diamonds State Park. We have a trailer we hitch up to Dad's truck. That way, our home is always with us, kind of like we're turtles!" Jenny said the last part bravely, as if having an old trailer to live in was somehow appealing.

"My goodness, I didn't know people could actually live at the Crater of Diamonds," said Grandma Jo.

Jenny shrugged. "I don't know about that, but Dad pays the park ranger our fees and we're set up to stay there for now."

Grandma got a faraway look on her face. "You know, it's been a long time since I was out to the park. When I was young, my friends and I would scoot out there and try to sneak into the mines to search for diamonds."

"Mines?" asked Jenny. "I thought there was just one place to look."

"Oh, goodness, no! You don't really think a volcano was going to spew up diamonds in just that thirty-seven acres they've got plowed out there, do you? Before it was a state park, that property was in a lot of different hands. When I was a young teenager, two different families owned it. One called their land The Diamond Preserve of the United States and the other called their property The Big Mine. They had billboards all over town advertising their properties and selling tickets to let people mine for diamonds. The Prairie Creek Pipe was big enough for us teenagers to snoop around, that's for sure!"

"Prairie Creek Pipe? What's that?" asked Jenny. "We cross Prairie Creek every day driving into town right by that spooky, old house on the hill. I know it connects on around to The Little Missouri River. What's the pipe?"

"Oh, honey, it isn't a pipe like you'd run water through or anything like that. A pipe is also a word to describe where lava flows out of a volcano."

Jenny and Kate reached for another round of gooey cookies straight from the oven. Grandma Jo gave them a look. "Have all you want, but don't get a stomachache!" The girls continued to munch contentedly and Grandma Jo continued. "You know, girls, looking over this list of minerals and hearing you talk about living at the Crater of Diamonds Park reminds me of a story."

Kate's eyes lit up. "Is it the one I'm thinking of, Grandma? You know, the one about the lost diamond?"

Grandma nodded. "The lost German diamond."

Jenny paused, a cookie almost to her mouth, "German diamond? What's that?"

"Well, the diamond really wasn't from Germany," answered Grandma Jo. "It was from here at our very own Crater of Diamonds. It was called the lost German diamond because of . . . wait," she broke off. "I'm getting ahead of myself. Let me start at the beginning."

5

"Jenny, what I'm about to tell you happened to my mother, Lucy Newberry, so I know the story is true. You hear lots of legends and stories around here with the Crater of Diamonds. After all, it is the only place in America where you can find diamonds like the ones found in the mines in Africa. A lot of the stories maybe started with a grain of truth and then got exaggerated." Grandma Jo paused dramatically, looking Jenny in the eye, "But this is the real deal. This is the story just as my mother told me. Imagine with me what it would have been like back in 1944. My mother, Lucy Newberry, decided to see the German soldiers who were being held prisoner here in our little town."

1944

"I'll be home for supper, Mother," Lucy called as she walked onto the front porch. The floor planks were painted a soft gray and the porch ceiling the soft blue of a freshly laid robin's egg. Mother swore by her blue paint, saying that it kept those pesky barn swallows from building one of their mud-laden nests on her clean, sunny porch. At one end of the porch was a swing filled with yellow-and-white checked toss pillows as stuffed as a Christmas goose. It was a perfect place to curl up with a favorite book.

Lucy had no interest in the porch swing today. She had someone she wanted to see and a mission to accomplish. What she'd failed to tell her mother was that she was headed to town to see if she could find where the prisoners were working today. Lucy had heard about the newest shipments of prisoners from Europe arriving to the prisoner of war camp yesterday, and she wanted to take a look.

She found something morbidly interesting about seeing these men who'd been captured by the Allied forces and shipped to the United States to their little town of Murfreesboro, Arkansas. There was something mysterious and fascinating about these men from homes and towns far away in the country of Germany across the Atlantic. Germany was where that awful Hitler was killing the Jews.

The prisoners had to live at the camp and work in the area until the war ended . . . whenever that would be. Lucy and her friend Susanna had taken a gander at the first busload of prisoners when they came in. Most of the men were her father's age, but a few of the soldiers were younger.

Lucy had listened as her dad talked at the supper table last night about the prisoners. "It is just plain disturbing to see young men locked up. Some of them don't appear to look any older than our Lucy here! Yet they've been on the battlefield and are now captured and stuck out here in southern Arkansas thousands of miles from home. It's just not right! This war needs to end, so people can reunite with their families and start rebuilding their lives."

Lucy knew that the POW camp was off limits for her and her friends, but she also knew some of the prisoners had been sent to work on repairing the brick paving of the streets around the county courthouse. It would be a perfect ruse to head over to Hawkins drugstore for an ice cream cone. The courthouse was right around the corner.

The sidewalk was rough in places, so she had to step carefully. Murfreesboro was a small town laid out in neatly organized squares as precise as a checkerboard. The only anomaly in the grid was the county courthouse and the drive that circled around it.

Hawkins' drugstore stood on a corner. The screen door creaked wildly on new springs as Lucy went in.

"What'll it be, Miss Lucy?" asked Mr. Hawkins. He was the only pharmacist in town but would dip the ice cream sometimes if the store wasn't too busy.

"I'll take a scoop of chocolate on a cone, please."

The exchange was made—one nickel for one cone of creamy, chocolate iciness, and Lucy was back out the door. "Thanks, Mr. Hawkins!" she called.

"You come again!"

Lucy let her tongue swirl over the top of the cone; the rich chocolate cooling her throat on the hot summer day.

She walked on around the square and heard them before she saw them—the crunch of the wheelbarrows on gravel, the murmured voices. Lucy rounded the corner and slowed her step. Some men were carefully placing paving bricks in order on the street. Others were lounging by a water tank, sipping from metal cups. Lucy felt brave with the guards nearby to protect her.

"Afternoon," she said to the three young men gathered at the water tank.

One replied, "Afternoon," only it sounded like "off noon." She flashed him a smile and hurried on past.

His blue eyes were seared in her mind, and she determined then and there to become friends with this German who was living in the POW camp on the northeast edge of town. Her father had talked about how wrong it was to keep these young men captured, and it seemed only right to her to befriend them. She glanced back one more time and caught the young prisoner's eye and then scooted safely on home.

——⬝⬝⬝——

At this point of the story Jenny and Kate were listening intently; the cookies long forgotten.

"I can't believe there were really prisoners of war right here in Murfreesboro!" exclaimed Jenny. "Where did they live?"

"Out near the Burger Barn," said Kate.

"The north side of town is where the prisoner of war camp was located in Murfreesboro," continued Grandma Jo.

"You see, there were thousands of German soldiers shipped to the United States to be held as prisoners of war. Evidently, there were too many to ship them to Great Britain, which was where they first sent the captured prisoners. As a backup plan, many prisoners were sent to the southern part of the United States. They kept the prisoners located in the southern states so it wouldn't cost so much to keep them warm during the winter months. Most of the prisoners sent to Arkansas were from the elite Afrika Korps. The train rolled into Murfreesboro in the spring of 1944 with about three hundred of the German soldiers. Most of the prisoners were sent to work in the Mississippi delta region of the state, so they could pick cotton."

"Did Lucy make friends with the soldier, Grandma Jo?" asked Jenny, forgetting to be shy.

"As a matter of fact, she eventually did. His name was Hans."

Kate leaned over. "Kind of a cool name, you know, like Hans Christian Andersen, the famous story writer."

Jenny nodded. "Did they ever get to just hang out and talk, or was he always locked up?"

"Well, you see, that is where the story gets interesting. My mother was never known for her patience or for listening to the advice of others. She started telling her parents, my grandparents, about Hans and how the soldiers were being treated. She would describe how they were poor boys far from home who had had to fight and serve in an awful war. My grandparents got so tired of hearing her complain that they finally decided they would do something to help the prisoners have a taste of home. I think they thought if they could show the town was friendly, somehow those prisoner soldiers would one day go back to Germany and tell about how wonderful

Americans really were. It was their attempt at world peace. Anyway, Lucy's parents and their friends organized a social to encourage the townsfolk to mingle with the German soldiers. Lucy worked with her mother to decorate the school gymnasium."

—ᴧᴧᴧ—

1944

The high school gymnasium was decorated with streamers, and long tables were set with punch bowls. Ice cream makers filled with homemade sweetness and wrapped in towels and ice were ready and waiting for the guests. Lucy was excited about the International Ice Cream Social. That's what the event was being called since it was a chance for the small town of Murfreesboro to show their southern hospitality to the visiting German prisoners. Mr. Nichols was playing his fiddle for background music, and the room was abuzz with excitement as the busload of prisoners of war was unloaded.

The young men stepping off the transport bus seemed hesitant and out of place in their drab khaki prison uniforms amidst all of the colorful dresses and neat shirts and neckties adorning the people of the community. The prisoners acted as uncomfortable as they looked.

Some people in town resented the German soldiers. There were folks who had their own sons fighting in the war and didn't appreciate the prisoners being treated like guests and that the social was held in their honor.

Lucy didn't care about all of the opinions. She just wanted to have a chance to visit with Hans. She caught sight of him looking awkwardly at the choices of ice cream, trying to make sense of some of the signs listing flavors. Walking up behind him, she pointed. "Try Mrs. Nichols' banana ice cream. It's the best in town."

Hans flashed Lucy a grateful smile and held out his dish to Mrs. Nichols. She scooped several spoonfuls of the banana treat into Hans' bowl.

"Thank you," he said to Mrs. Nichols and then turned to Lucy. "Your name? I saw you when I working on street? My name Hans." He said the words slowly, testing his English skills.

"Lucy Newberry." She extended her right hand. "My parents are the ones who put this social together. We want you to feel more welcome in our community."

"Thank you," answered Hans, continuing in his faltering English. "It kind of you. We do similar thing in my village. Women bring best strudel for all to taste and then one gets blue ribbon. My mother won blue ribbon before war." At that comment, his face became awash in sadness.

"Mother alone now. Father killed in battle. I glad when I can someday go home and help with farm."

As they talked, Lucy discovered Hans was only a couple of years older than her. He told Lucy that he had lied about his age when he enlisted in the army. He was just a lonely kid who needed a friend. She was fascinated to hear about what it was like to grow up in a German village instead of a small town in Arkansas.

"Where have you been working since you finished the road? I haven't seen any of you working around town lately."

Hans tasted his first spoonful of Mrs. Nichols' banana ice cream. He closed his eyes as he savored the bite, "This good! We have nothing like it in my country."

He smiled at Lucy. "They move us to work diamond field and mine. Your government think if we find diamonds, it raise money for war against us. We find small stones. Not worth much."

"I've always wanted to go out to where the diamond mine is, but they keep things pretty locked up around there," said Lucy. "They don't encourage any kind of visitors. You'll have to let me know if you find anything. That would be so exciting!"

Hans smiled. "Thank you, Lucy, for your kindness. Thank your parents. I would like to call you friend."

"Of course, I will be your friend." Lucy noticed that Hans had finished his dish of ice cream and pointed to where the punch bowls and pitchers

of water were set out. "If you are thirsty, just go over there and the ladies will take care of you. In fact, the woman wearing the yellow dress is my mother."

———∞———

"Goodness, look at the time!" exclaimed Grandma Jo. "Jenny, your dad is probably worried about you."

Jenny looked at the clock on the mint green wall. It showed five thirty. "I do need to go," she said. "Dad was working an extra hour overtime today, but I need to get over to the sawmill." She rose from the chair to go; the back of her legs sticking to the red vinyl cushion. "Thanks, Grandma Jo, for the cookies. And for telling me the story," she added.

"You come back again, okay?" asked Grandma Jo. "There is more of the story to tell."

"I'll see," replied Jenny. Then with another look at the clock, she waved goodbye to Kate and took off down the street as quickly as she could go without running and drawing attention to herself. She felt a bit like a modern-day Cinderella knowing that her dad would be full of too many questions if she wasn't waiting for him in the truck. She hadn't told Dad about her plan to go to Kate's house after school.

The familiar blue truck was a welcome sight as Jenny rounded the corner near the mill. She didn't know what her father would ever do if she wasn't waiting on him. She'd never had to worry about it before, but now that she had a friend with Kate and was making more friends at school, she might have to talk with him about sometimes picking her up at Grandma Jo's house. The thought made her shudder. She'd rather not have him showing up in this junky truck.

She'd hardly gotten into the cab of the truck and locked the door behind her when Dad came out of the mill. "Hi, Jenny," he said, pounding his hello on the hood as he reached the driver's door, "Sorry you had to wait so long today. How was school?"

Jenny gave a shrug. "Fine, I guess," she replied. She decided not to mention Kate or Grandma Jo just yet.

They rode along in silence as they went through town. Jenny could tell something was on her father's mind. He was uncharacteristically quiet. He looked over at Jenny and began to speak, "I called your school today."

Jenny felt a lurch in her stomach. What did this mean? Were they moving again?

6

Jenny stared at Dad as he drove, worried to hear what he would say.

He continued, "I called to see if the school bus will take you home from school. I found out this morning that I can work more overtime at the mill, and it would help us get ahead. But, I hate to think of you having to sit in the truck for so long every day."

"How late would you have to work?" asked Jenny, breathing a thank you prayer under her breath, relieved that he hadn't said they were moving.

"Most days I'd be finished up by six thirty. It's still light outside this time of year, so you could go on home to the RV and do any homework and get some dinner fixed. That is, if you'd want to do that. If you want to stay in the truck, that's fine, but I think you'd be plenty safe at the park. There really aren't many people around now that school is in session, and the park ranger on duty is always patrolling."

Jenny thought through the new situation. She really didn't want to have to sit in the pickup truck every day for over two hours. The fact that her dad wanted to do the extra work and had the opportunity was a good thing given how far they'd fallen behind in their stash of cash as her dad liked to call it.

But the thought of being alone out at the state park sounded a little scary. They only had one cell phone, and her dad kept it with him.

"What would I do if I needed help for anything? You have the phone."

"I thought about that," said Dad. "The visitor center is just down the path a couple of hundred yards. The park rangers and staff stay there at least until five thirty and then there is always a ranger on patrol in the park around the clock. I figure if you stay close to the RV, you'll be fine. And remember, there is a pay phone up by the restrooms. We could make sure you have plenty of quarters handy in case you need to call me. Of course, this is only if you want to do it. You are welcome to still wait for me in the truck."

Jenny had a frown on her face as she continued to think through this new option. "What about Whiskers?"

Whiskers was the nickname of the wizened old man they had seen in the park every day since they'd arrived. Jenny was sure it was him who had stared them down that first morning. It appeared as if he mined the plowed diamond field every day until park closing time.

"Whiskers? I don't think you need to worry about him. I admit he's a scruffy looking man, but I think the only thing he's interested in is searching for diamonds. He must leave every day when the field closes because I know we haven't seen him around here later in the evenings."

"He's kind of weird-looking with the pack he has on his back and that scraggly beard," said Jenny. Whiskers had a black beard that was almost striped with gray. Jenny had never seen anything like it.

Dad gave a snort. "Yeah, who would have thought of using swimming pool noodles to make a cushion for his backpack straps? It's actually a pretty clever idea if you ask me. I bet he doesn't get very tired hauling the pack all day while he's searching for diamonds." Jenny still had a worried look on her face.

"I really don't think you have anything to be uneasy about, but I can ask the ranger about him. Here's the deal. The bus does make a stop near the entrance for the children who live near the trading post down the road past the park. The man who is in charge of busing told me there is a trail that runs up behind the trading store that leads into the woods by where we camp. So you could use the trail instead of having to walk on the main roads."

Jenny turned away from her father, watching the woods flash by as they drove into the park. She was fearful of reading his face. "What are you planning to do when you make the extra money? Do you want to stay here or move again?" When he paused, she turned back around to watch his reaction to her questions.

"Well," he said, glancing at her, "I'm thinking about staying here for awhile. My boss at the mill has been real nice, and you've talked about how much you like school. I thought we might be able to stay here at least through the end of the year. But, I don't know how cold it will get starting in January, so we may have to move somewhere farther south when you are out for Christmas break. If it gets too cold, we can't stay in the RV because I can't afford to run the heater all the time. We'll just have to wait and see."

Her heart sank. Even though it would be wonderful to stay in the school through Christmas, possibly the longest time they'd ever stayed in one place, she wished they could stay put for good. If only her father could make enough money to rent a little place in town. She thought about the Crater of Diamonds. Even though Dad would be too tired to look for diamonds with the extra work hours at the mill, maybe she could search for them when she got home from school. After all, now she had an idea of what to do since she'd searched at Ka-Do-Ha. She wouldn't have to tell her dad what she was up to. Who knows, maybe she could find something of value that would help their family finances. Maybe they could stay in Murfreesboro forever!

Jenny liked thinking about searching for a valuable diamond but didn't know what she thought about having to be alone in the park. But, she reasoned, if she were busy digging for diamonds, she'd at least be doing something for their situation instead of hanging around in a pickup truck. Maybe, just maybe, if she could find a diamond worth some real money, they could move into that rental house in town Grandma Jo mentioned, the Garrison house, and they could just stay in Murfreesboro. Jenny made her decision.

"I'm okay with riding the bus home," she told Dad. "I'm sure I'll be just fine."

As Jim Shoemaker pulled into their campsite, he looked over at his daughter. "I know you'll be fine," he assured her. He shifted the truck's gear into park. "Let's eat. Tomorrow is payday, so we only have to have macaroni and cheese one more evening for our supper. Plan on waiting for me in the truck one last time tomorrow, and we'll go to the grocery store to get our food. Before we grocery shop, though, we'll stop and get a couple of burgers at the Burger Barn for a treat to celebrate my overtime pay!"

7

Friday made the top ten list of good days for Jenny. As soon as Mrs. Lancaster had given them the sheet of notebook paper for the mineral quiz, Jenny penciled in TGCFAOQTCD at the top of the paper. Then she thought carefully of each mineral that the letters represented. Grandma Jo was right. By having the clever acronym Tall Giants Can Find An Orange Quacking Tiny Colorful Duck, Jenny was able to remember all of the minerals. She got a hundred on the quiz. And at the end of the day, she won the drawing of the week for her good behavior. As she returned from picking out a new spiral notebook as her reward, Kate gave her a thumbs-up. Leaning over as Jenny walked by, she whispered, "Want to come over again today?"

Jenny eyes brightened, and she gave a quick nod, knowing she wouldn't start riding the bus home until next week.

Once Mrs. Lancaster dismissed the class, the two girls took off to walk the three blocks to Grandma Jo's. "Do you think your grandma is going to tell us the rest of the story about Lucy today?" asked Jenny.

"If you ask her. She loves to tell the story of that lost diamond."

The girls opened the screen door to sweet and spicy smells. Grandma Jo came around the corner from the kitchen into the living room, "Jenny!" she exclaimed warmly. "I'm so glad you were able to come back over." She gave Jenny a little hug. "Is this all right with your father for you to come by for a snack?"

Jenny gave a nod. "He's fine with it. I just need to leave here by five fifteen at the latest." *Of course*, thought Jenny, *what Dad doesn't know won't hurt him.*

"Great," replied Grandma Jo. "Come in the kitchen, girls. I made some oatmeal raisin cookies. I added a little more cinnamon than my typical recipe calls for, and I think they are delicious!"

Following the earlier routine, the girls set their backpacks near the back door and washed up. This time, Grandma Jo poured full glasses of sweet tea and placed a platter of the warm cookies on the table between them.

Jenny took her first bite and closed her eyes. "Grandma Jo, these have got to be the best cookies I've ever eaten!" she exclaimed. "They're so chewy and sweet!"

Grandma Jo smiled at Jenny's reaction. "Glad you like 'em, honey," she replied. "What about you, Kate? You've had my other recipe. Do you like these better or the old ones?"

Kate was chewing and held up her finger to signal Grandma Jo to wait. Following a drink of tea, she answered, "These definitely! They are amazing. You'll have to show me what you did, so I can learn to bake these, too!"

Jenny looked back and forth at Grandma Jo and Kate. What would it be like to live in a house and be able to bake cookies and do your homework on the worn Formica top of a real kitchen table, not on one that folded into a bed? The trailer she and Dad lived in was a far cry from this charming small house in town.

Kate shared a look with Jenny. "Grandma, will you tell us the rest of Lucy's story? You know, about the diamond? Jenny would like to hear the rest of it."

Grandma Jo gave the girls a smile. "Of course, I'll be happy to tell you about the German diamond as we call it in our family. I think I left the story yesterday telling you about the social, right?"

The girls nodded eagerly. "Well, after the social, the townsfolk were a lot friendlier with the German prisoners of war. People in town started to appreciate the prisoners working. They realized many jobs now being done by the prisoners had been neglected after so many of the local boys and men had enlisted to go fight in the war. Having the prisoners around town pretty much became a way of life. You might see some of them working on the roads in town, and then you'd see yellow school buses loaded with some of them being transported out of town to the diamond mining area. My mother told me of her friendship with Hans.

"One industry that the government tried to restart was diamond mining. They believed it might help raise money for the war effort."

Kate wiggled her eyebrows at Jenny. "This is where the story starts to get interesting," she interrupted. "Go on, Grandma Jo, tell her about the diamond."

"Ah, surely I'm boring you girls with all of this old history."

"No," interjected Jenny. "I think it is so interesting! I can't believe there are diamonds right here in Arkansas. Did Kate tell you I found a diamond at Ka-Do-Ha on our field trip?"

Grandma Jo nodded. "She did mention it to me. Your diamond probably came from the same soil as the German diamond."

"So what is the story, Grandma Jo?"

"Well, armed guards were hired at the diamond mine to keep the German prisoners from stealing any stones they found. The armed guards patrolled the mining company by walking on the ceiling trusses above where the prisoners of war were sifting for diamonds. The guards were supposed to keep an eye on the prisoners to make sure they didn't pocket anything of value.

"As it turns out, the young German soldier my mother was friends with, Hans, discovered a special diamond, a really large one. It was so large he knew it was valuable, and he didn't want to turn it in to his supervisor. After all, he reasoned, if he kept it, he could take it with him back to Germany and help his family rebuild after World War II was over.

"He managed to hide the stone without the guards or any other prisoners seeing him. He didn't tell any of his fellow prisoners about it, fearful they might steal it from him or report his theft."

"Did he get to take the stone with him when he left, Grandma Jo?" asked Jenny.

"No, that's the sad part of this story. You see, the war was coming to a close in the spring of 1945 with the unconditional surrender of Germany. The government started shipping out the prisoners of war back to their home countries. One day, the prisoners at Murfreesboro were loaded, without warning, onto the trains and shipped to the East Coast where they could board ships that would take them home. It seems as if Hans didn't have the opportunity to go get the diamond from where he hid it. Obviously, he couldn't admit he had the stone because he might have been imprisoned for the theft. He had to leave it behind."

"Isn't this sad, Jenny?" asked Kate. "Every time I hear Grandma Jo tell the story, I'm always so sad for Hans and how he had to go back to his family empty-handed when he could have been able to help them so much."

Jenny nodded as Grandma continued. "Several months after Hans and the other prisoners were gone, my mother, Lucy, received a letter from Hans. In it he told her about the diamond and asked if she could help him find it. He suggested that if she could find the stone, they could share in the value of it. He told Lucy to take it to a jeweler to be cut once she found it and then to send him half of the money.

"Lucy was confident she could find the stone. His directions and clues seemed so clear. She wrote back to Hans telling him that she would help him. She knew she'd have to keep her parents from finding out what she was doing because they would feel as if she should keep all of the money from the stone rather than sharing it with a prisoner."

"Did she find it? Did she send him the money?" asked Jenny.

Grandma Jo shook her head. "No, unfortunately, the story didn't end happily. Lucy looked everywhere that Hans' clues led her to but with no luck. She never found the diamond. She finally told her father about the letter from Hans and showed it to him. He helped her look as well but they hit a dead end every time. They finally decided that someone else amongst the prisoners must have found the diamond and kept it. That, it seems, is the end of the story."

"But what if no one ever found it? What if it is still in Hans' hiding place?" cried Jenny.

Kate shook her head. "How could it possibly still be around? There's no way it is still in some random hiding place."

"Why not? There's no proof that someone else found it. I wish I could have read Hans' letter to Lucy. I bet we could have figured it out."

Grandma Jo had a smile on her face. "Really, Jenny, you think you could figure it out if you could read the letter?"

Jenny nodded. "I bet we could. Don't you think so, Kate?"

Kate nodded her head. "Of course, we could, Grandma Jo. You know what smart girls we are! At least you are always telling me how smart I am!" This time, Kate gave Grandma Jo a teasing glance.

"Well, you two smartypants," she said. "We'll just see how clever you are!" Grandma Jo walked out of the cherry-themed mint green and red kitchen and left Kate and Jenny seated at the gray and white swirled Formica table.

"What do you think she's up to?" asked Jenny.

Kate shrugged. "I have no idea what she's doing. Do you want another cookie?" Jenny nodded, picked up one that was dotted with chewy raisins, and bit into it slowly.

"These are pure heaven, Kate, you know it?" asked Jenny as she wiped the crumbs off her lip with a napkin.

"They are good," agreed Kate. "I guess when you have something all the time, it isn't quite as special as when you have it for the first time."

"Here, girls!" cried Grandma Jo as she reentered the small kitchen. "Let's see how good you are at figuring out clues." Grandma smiled as she laid a worn envelope on the kitchen table.

"What's this, Grandma?" asked Kate. Then she looked at the envelope more carefully. "Is this what I think it is?"

"What?" asked Jenny excitedly, "What is it?"

"It's Lucy's letter from the German soldier," said Grandma Jo. "We'll see how well you do with figuring out the lost diamond, girls."

Jenny couldn't believe that Grandma Jo had the letter from Hans here at the house. Even more, she couldn't understand why they hadn't searched for the diamond before now.

Grandma Jo carefully opened the envelope and unfolded the fragile yellowed piece of paper. "Let's read it together, girls," she said.

"Dear Lucy, I hope your family *gut*."

"Gut! That's gross, why would he say that to her after they had become friends?" asked Jenny.

Grandma Jo gave a smile. "Gut in German means good. He is saying that he hopes that she and her family are good, you know, like doing okay. Obviously he didn't master the entire English language while he was here. You have to remember he wrote this letter after he'd been back to Germany for awhile. He'd probably forgotten some of the English he'd learned here."

Jenny gave a nod, and Grandma Jo continued reading the letter. "I have return to my country, and it sad to see. Many families are without homes. My family have home, but barn torn down to get wood for fire during winter. My mother alive, but two of my brother killed in battle along with Father."

"How sad," said Kate, "to go home and to have everything so changed."

Grandma read on, "We try to survive. We have a few chicken that lay eggs my mother sell in village. I work to rebuild houses and buildings in town.

"I write to see if you will help since you are *freund*. I did not tell you this while in your town. I find diamond while working in mine. It large, and I hid it to take to my home country. They load us on train before I could get it.

"My family need money the diamond could bring. Can you search for me? If you find it, I happy to share the *knete*, the money, from it. Would you do this for me, your German soldier friend? Our families would *der vorteil*.

"My English better from living in your village but still not best. Please forgive. I don't know who will be reading this. You must think carefully. Be wise in search."

The following words were listed across the bottom of the page: *diamant, boden, ecke, fundament, baum, diamant.*

"These are all in German," said Jenny, her voice laced with disappointment. "How are we supposed to understand them?"

"Well, I did look them up a long time ago, but none of it made sense to me, so I gave up on trying to do anything with it. The words are diamond, ground, corner, base, tree, diamond."

Kate and Jenny exchanged a look, and then Jenny asked, "Do you have a piece of paper where I could write this down?"

"Sure," replied Grandma Jo. She took a cherry-rimmed magnetic notepad off the refrigerator door and gave it to Jenny. "Write away!"

Jenny carefully copied the words and tore off the sheet. Then she rewrote the list again and gave Kate that copy. "Here you go," she said to Grandma Jo, handing her the pad and pen. "Thank you."

Jenny looked at the clock on the kitchen wall. She hadn't noticed before, but even it had cherries on it instead of numbers. "Gosh! I've got to go. We're going to eat at the Burger Barn tonight."

"Look over the clues this weekend," said Kate. "I will, too. Who knows, maybe with some fresh eyes, we might figure out the mystery."

Jenny nodded. "I will. Thanks, Grandma Jo, for the cookies!" With a quick wave, Jenny bounded down the steps and began her walk to the mill; the list of German words clutched tightly in her fist.

Her mind was racing as she approached the mill. If the diamond had been hidden near where the soldiers were mining, that wouldn't be too far from where their RV was camped. Riding the bus home from school, she'd have time to search each day without anyone knowing. Maybe Kate could come home with her, and somehow they could search together.

Wouldn't it be wonderful if they could find the diamond? Then maybe she and Dad could stay in Murfreesboro for good.

8

The weekend had been a good one. Dad had kept his promise to have dinner at the Burger Barn. Then they'd stocked up on groceries. After so many days of macaroni and cheese or hot dogs and baked beans, the cheeseburger and French fries had tasted heavenly. They'd finished their dinners with chocolate shakes complete with whipped cream.

All weekend, Jenny studied the list of German words. Surely she could figure out the clues!

When Monday morning rolled around, Jenny was more than ready to get back to school. She was eager to see if Kate had any luck trying to figure out what the words might mean. Even though she looked forward to being at school, she dreaded riding the bus home later that afternoon. She knew she should be safe in their trailer at the park, but that did little to relieve her anxiety about being alone and not having a phone if she needed something. On Sunday, Dad had walked the path with her to the visitor center and park ranger station and reminded her that they would be open until five thirty.

Mrs. Lancaster was all business, getting the class started on their weekly routine, and so the girls didn't have a chance to talk until lunch. While they were eating, Kate pulled out her list of German words. Heads together, seated at one end of a table in the cafeteria, they began to discuss their ideas.

"Hey, what's this!" yelled Tim, snatching the list out of Kate's hand. They were so engrossed in their conversation they hadn't even noticed him sneaking up on them.

"Give that back, Tim Grimes!" yelled Kate, jumping off of her chair to try to get the list back.

Tim paused to look at what he grabbed. He snorted, "Looks like a bunch of gobbly-gook to me. What do you think this is, Ben?" His buddy looked at the list and shrugged. Even though he remained silent, it was obvious he was highly amused by Kate and Jenny's distress over their list being taken by the smirk on his face.

This time, Kate lowered her voice. "Give me my paper, Tim Grimes, or else I'll . . ."

"Or else you'll what, Kate? Go tattle on me? Like I even care!"

Tim took off, triumphantly waving the clues above his head, grinning back wickedly at the girls.

Jenny was worried. "Kate, we've got to do something! We can't let him look for the diamond!" Then after a moment she added, "He's always so annoying! I've met his dad at the small grocery store."

Kate nodded. "Yeah, Mr. Grimes is his dad. To hear Grandma Jo talk about them, the Grimes are nothing but trouble around town. Tim Grimes has been a pest to me since he stole my favorite pencil in kindergarten and then pulled out the eraser."

Jenny smiled a second, imagining a miniature freckle-faced Kate upset with round-faced Tim. She couldn't imagine what it would be like to attend the same school long enough to know everyone since they'd started kindergarten.

Kate continued, "He doesn't know that the words are related to the missing German diamond. I'm going to pretend like it doesn't matter and more than likely he'll give it back, or at least quit hounding us about it. As soon as I get all paranoid and in a panic, he'll figure out that he has something important, and then we *will* have to worry about what he might do."

Even though it concerned Jenny, Kate made sense. It had been Jenny's experience in all of the many schools she had attended in her short life that bullies could best be dealt with if she acted as if she didn't care about their actions towards her.

"Plus," continued Kate, "we still have the original letter and the copy you made of the words." She looked across the lunchroom and saw that Tim had gone outside to the playground to find fresh meat to torment.

"You've studied the list, Jenny. What do you think the words mean?"

"Well," Jenny began, "you know that we live in our trailer out at the Crater of Diamonds Park. This weekend while I was hanging out in the park laundromat washing our clothes, I picked up a camp brochure that had a map of the park. According to the map, the area where they used to have the commercial diamond mine was on the south side of the park, near Prairie Creek. I wonder if the corner he talks about is maybe a cornerstone of the old mining building.

"Same with the word, base. You know, he might have been referring to the base of the building and that the diamond was hidden in a corner of the building near the ground, or maybe buried in the ground near the base of the building. And the tree is a real mystery because the whole area is full of trees. We can hardly see the sun overhead in the middle of the afternoon at our campsite because the trees are so thick."

"You might be onto something, Jenny, tying his word choices to the mine since we know that he was working there every day before they shipped him back to Germany."

Jenny had never considered inviting someone, anyone, to come near their rickety, old trailer, but an idea was starting to brew. She wanted to share the search for the diamond with Kate. She decided not to worry anymore about the RV and how it looked. Kate was her friend and hopefully she wouldn't judge her by that.

"Kate," she paused. "I don't know if this would work or not, but my dad said I could start riding the bus home to the park after school instead of going to the mill and waiting for him every day until he is finished with work.

"What would you think about coming home with me once in awhile in the afternoons? We could search for the diamond before he gets home from the mill. The park is pretty empty now, and the official mining area closes by four thirty, so by the time we'd get there, we'd pretty much have the park to ourselves. It doesn't get dark until close to seven."

Kate's eyes lit up. "That's a perfect idea!" she squealed. Then her face turned serious. "The trick is in figuring out how to get out there and then back home without Grandma

Jo becoming suspicious about what we are up to." She paused as the bell rang to signal the students to line up to go back to class for the afternoon. She turned back to Jenny. "I'll think about it. Talk to you after school!"

The afternoon drug on in class. Both girls found it hard to concentrate. Any time Jenny had to walk by Tim in class, he would smirk at her as if he was mocking her. Once he laid the word list on the edge of his desk as Jenny walked by just to tease her. She glared at him but didn't say a word. Kate was right. He didn't have a clue what the words were about, and she wasn't going to give him the time of day.

When the bell rang, she and Kate were the first to leave the classroom. "What do you think, Kate?" asked Jenny. "How can we get you out to the park to help me search?"

"I was trying to come up with ideas. I think I can maybe ride the bus home with you some days. We can tell Grandma Jo that we have a science project of gathering stones for our mineral study at school. It's a perfect idea since you live at the park for us to search around there to find some of the cool crystals that are often found at the Crater in addition to the diamonds. We'll let her know that your dad said it would be okay for us to be in the park to do our searching. If she thinks he is fine with it, she would probably make the drive out to pick me up. I would ride the bus home with you those days. We'd tell the bus driver we were working on a project. I wouldn't be able to come out every day since I have piano lessons and soccer practice some days. But at least we could look together a couple days a week. The other days you'd be on your own to search."

Jenny nodded her head thoughtfully. "That might work. My dad wouldn't have to do any driving and that would be a good thing because he'd get upset if he thought I was asking him to waste gas. Ask Grandma Jo about it tonight, and see if she'll agree to the idea. Tell her the park is really safe, the park rangers are always on patrol, and there are hardly any outside campers there at this time of the year." Jenny decided not to mention old Whiskers.

"Will do," said Kate. "If we're lucky, we might be able to start looking tomorrow." The girls shared a grin.

They each headed off in their separate directions. Today though, Jenny followed the students who were headed to the lineup of yellow school buses. Her step was a little lighter. If she and Kate could find the lost diamond, it would solve so many of their problems. She and her dad would no longer have to worry about having enough money. And maybe, just maybe, if her dad felt like he had enough money, he would stay in one place, and she could call Murfreesboro her permanent home.

9

Lining up to board the bus, Jenny noted that Zack from her class was also with her group. She didn't know he lived out her way. She wasn't sure how she felt having him ride her bus. He'd been rude to her the day of the field trip. He'd more or less left her alone since then, and she hoped he wouldn't start bothering her on the bus.

"Hey, Jenny," Zack said as he came up behind her to board the bus. "I didn't know you lived out by me."

"Where do you live?" she asked.

"At the trading post. It's down the road past the state park."

Jenny gave Zack a small smile. She wasn't keen on telling him where she lived but realized it would be next to impossible to keep it a secret since they would be on the same bus route. "Well, I actually live at the state park. We have an RV there."

There, she'd said it. She waited for him to come back with some smart reply, but instead he just nodded his head. "I live in the trailer park that's by the trading post. Have you been there yet?"

Jenny shook her head. "My dad and I drove by it, but we didn't stop to go in."

The two started making their way to the middle of the bus. As Jenny went to sit down, she was surprised that Zack took the seat next to her. "My grandparents run the trading post, and my mom works there to help them out. We get to live in our trailer rent-free since the land belongs to my grandparents. It's not the best setup, but at least it's home. I just try to steer clear of all the tourists who come around in the summer."

Jenny was surprised Zack lived in a trailer. For some reason, she'd visualized everyone in class living in a house except for her. She didn't say much more but instead looked out the window of the bus, taking in the familiar sights. As the bus rounded the bend before reaching Prairie Creek, she turned to Zack. "There," she said as she pointed. "That house. Tell me, what is it? It looks so big and spooky."

A large house loomed on the north side of the road. Off to the left, standing two stories tall, the house had an extra box-like structure on top.

"Oh, the Mauney House," said Zack. "You're right. It is kind of spooky looking. It's been empty for years."

"Well, it gives me the shivers every time my dad and I drive by it."

"It's the oldest standing building in Pike County," Zack continued. "My parents have told me that the house was built by a man named Isaac Mauney. See that top part?" He pointed to the top of the house. "The story goes that the top was used as an Indian lookout. If they felt that there might be an uprising with the Indians who lived nearby, Isaac would go up there with other family members to keep watch. By looking out all the windows, they could tell if anyone was anywhere close to attacking them. It must have worked"—Zach shrugged—"because the house is still standing almost two hundred years later. Now people say it's haunted. There are lights on inside it some nights."

Jenny pressed her face closer to the window. The part on top made sense now although she hadn't known that Indians had lived in the area. She imagined what it would have been like living there almost two hundred years ago, long before John Huddleston ever discovered the first diamond in 1906. It was hard to imagine. Lost in thought, she didn't even realize they'd come to their stop.

Zack turned to her. "Come on, Jenny, this is our stop."

Jenny gathered her backpack and followed Zack off the bus. A few other students exited as well, but they were either older or younger, and she didn't recognize them from school. Once off the bus, she looked around, trying to get her bearings.

"So you live in the state park, right?" asked Zack. Jenny nodded. Zack pointed to an opening along the tree line at the base of the mountain. "That is the start of the trail that goes up into the park. Where exactly do you live in there?"

"Our campsite is on this end of the park. Dad and I looked over the trails this weekend. Our campsite is near where State Park Road meets Crater Road."

Zack nodded. "If that is where your RV is, then you'll be fine. Just follow that trail on up." He paused, seeming a little unsure of himself. "If you feel like you need anything, you could come back down here since my grandparents keep the trading post open until dusk." Zack gave a small smile.

Jenny smiled back. She hadn't been expecting to make a friend with Zack, but it appeared as if that was what was happening, and she was fine with it. She'd never really had friends before with all of their moves. Now she only hoped even more that she could find the lost German diamond, so she and her dad would have enough money that they could stay and live in Murfreesboro. Nothing would please her more than getting to live in one place and never having to move again.

With a quick wave of her hand, Jenny set off up the trail into the wooded park. Her dad had cautioned her to take her time and to be on the lookout for any wildlife that might be near the trails. They both had talked that even though it would feel almost as if she was walking in a jungle, it would feel less secluded once the trees started to lose their leaves in late October. However, now in September, the plants and trees were still green and lush. Fortunately, Jenny knew how to steer clear of poison oak and poison ivy.

The forest was quiet, and Jenny could hear herself breathing and her footsteps crunching along the gravel on the trail. She had to give herself a little pep talk. "Keep going, no reason to be afraid, everything will be fine." Keeping on the trail, Jenny watched for animals. They should scurry away if they saw or sensed her.

A flash of pink caught her eye. With a start, she peered closer into the woods but realized whatever she'd seen was gone. Her mind quickly thought of old Whiskers with his pink pool noodles strapped onto the ancient oversized camping backpack he kept over his shoulders. Even though Dad thought he was no one to worry about, Jenny knew she'd feel uneasy if she ran into him while she was home alone.

Jenny fingered the keys around her neck. They felt heavy. She had to admit that if she could get over being alone out here at the state park, it sure beat sitting in Dad's truck waiting for him every day.

Worried that Zack had sent her on the wrong trail, she was relieved as she came out of the trail onto the State Park Road. Crossing the road, she walked on another trail that led on up to their campsite. For the first time in her life, the RV looked good to her. She'd made it home without any incident. Hopefully tomorrow Kate would be able to come home with her, and they could start looking for the lost diamond. Jenny unlocked the door of the RV and let herself in. The vehicle felt strange. She realized it was the first time she'd ever been there without her dad to keep her company. To get over her uneasiness, she talked to herself and got busy organizing ingredients for dinner on the crowded counter. Dad would be home soon.

10

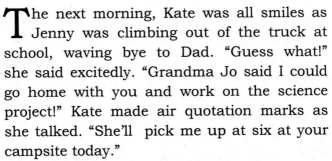

The next morning, Kate was all smiles as Jenny was climbing out of the truck at school, waving bye to Dad. "Guess what!" she said excitedly. "Grandma Jo said I could go home with you and work on the science project!" Kate made air quotation marks as she talked. "She'll pick me up at six at your campsite today."

The girls exchanged a grin. Today would be their day to start the search for the lost German diamond! Usually, Mrs. Lancaster kept a quick pace in the classroom, but the morning seemed to drag along. At lunch, Tim Grimes circled their table like a hawk while holding the list of word clues just above their reach.

"So, what is this, Kate?" he asked. "What makes it so important?"

"Give it to me, Tim, or—"

"Or what, Kate, what big bad thing are you going to do to me?"

Kate was fuming by now. "I'll just march over to the store and tell your dad about what you're doing, that's what!"

"I already showed my dad your little piece of paper."

At that comment, the two girls exchanged a frightened glance.

"He couldn't tell what it was about either," Tim leaned in closer. "But I'll figure it out. After all, it has diamond written on it, and everyone in town has heard the legend of the lost German diamond that your Grandma likes to talk about." Tim spun around and walked off.

Jenny's heart sunk further. "Kate, you didn't tell me that everyone in town knows about the German diamond!" she whispered sharply. "I thought we were the only ones who knew!"

"Don't worry about it, Jenny," Kate reassured her. "The story of the German diamond is just like all the other legends that have been floating around town for years. There's one story about a tobacco pouch of diamonds that was found in the roots of a tree, another was about a miner who worked the diamond field every day and found a diamond as long as his finger, but then it washed away into the mud. He looked for it for years, and others have searched that same creek bed with no luck.

"After so many years, the stories stretch and make for great tales to tell the tourists at the visitor center or at Buddy's Restaurant in town. But none of us who actually live here have an expectation that the stories are true. The advantage we have with our information is that we know it is true since it happened to my great grandma, Lucy Newberry. We just have to keep our search quiet."

"I hope Tim will leave us alone," said Jenny.

"He does enjoy picking on people, but as long as we don't let him know how much he's getting to us, he'll finally back off and leave us alone." Seeing the look of concern still on Jenny's face, she added, "Trust me, we've been in class together since kindergarten. I have a pretty good idea of how he operates."

The afternoon went by a little quicker, and finally the long-awaited dismissal bell rang. The school bus driver, Joe, nodded at Kate as she hopped on the bus with Jenny. "Project," was all she said with a warm smile, and that seemed to be the magic word. Zack swung onto the bus and gave a quick smile to the two girls and sat down on the row behind them.

The ride from town to the state park was only seven miles, so it didn't take too long even though there were a few stops to drop off children. As they neared Prairie Creek and the looming Mauney House, Jenny pointed it out. "Zack was telling me about that house yesterday on the way home."

Kate said, "Yeah, the old Mauney House. We've always stayed away from there. I think it's supposed to be haunted.

"See those windows on that part up high? Supposedly that is where the family had a lookout in case there was an Indian attack." Kate shivered. "It's hard to believe sometimes that where we live now could have been a dangerous place to live long ago."

"I know, I thought the same thing when Zack told me about the house."

"That would be scary, having to worry about having someone attacking your home. No one lives there anymore. It's empty, but I've heard that if you look in the windows, you can see some of the murals that were painted on the walls by one of the owners. A man named Isaac White built the house. Later, one of the Mauneys bought the house and had murals painted on the walls to show his childhood years, and he even had all kinds of log furniture built to put in the house. We learned about this last year in school," she added as an afterthought. "Sometimes the older kids talk about it and say they've seen lights in the windows when they drive out at night, but no one is supposed to be in there."

Jenny gave a little shiver. "I don't want to think about people being out here who shouldn't be. Especially since I'm out here for awhile every day until Dad gets home from the mill."

The bus pulled past the entrance of the park and stopped at the trading post. Zack got off the bus with Kate and Jenny and the other children who lived at the stop. "This is where we go," said Jenny, pointing to the worn path to the right. "I took this yesterday." She nodded to Zack. "Zack was nice enough to show me the right way to go, so I wouldn't get lost in the woods." She gave Zack a smile.

Zack gave them a wave, and the girls started up the path. The woods were thick as a wall as the girls walked along. As they pushed up the hillside, they could no longer see the trading post below or the campsite up ahead. Even though Jenny had walked it the day before, it felt as if they were lost in a thicket of green.

"Are you *sure* this is the right path?" asked Kate as they pushed ahead.

"Trust me, it is," replied Jenny. "It looks like we're lost, but really our campsite is just a few steps away. You'll see."

They went on ahead for a few more yards and then stepped out onto the side of the road. "See," said Jenny, "we've got to cross over the road to that last trail and we'll be there." The girls traveled along the rest of the trail without seeing anyone. The only sound was a squirrel scolding them from above. "There's our trailer."

"Come on, let's go inside, and you can see how I live." Jenny spoke in a joking tone to cover her anxiousness to see how Kate would react to the trailer. Grandma Jo's house was so nice, and looking at the trailer through the eyes of a visitor, Jenny knew it was lacking. She'd done her best to straighten and clean things up over the weekend, but no amount of cleaning can cover old and ugly. Jenny glanced over at Kate, trying to gauge her reaction.

"Sounds good," said Kate as she waited for Jenny to unlock the door. As the girls went inside, Kate commented on how cozy the trailer felt, but that was it. Jenny gave a sigh of relief. Her friend wasn't going to dump her just because she lived in a dump!

Gathering some snacks and throwing tools into Jenny's backpack, the girls locked up the trailer and took off. Jenny had the park trail map she'd picked up at the ranger station over the weekend. Based on Hans' note, they figured they should head through the woods to the west. Kate had asked Grandma Jo about it over dinner and thought she knew where she and Jenny should go to get to the old mine and washing company site. The park would be closing soon, and Jenny hoped that the park rangers wouldn't be on patrol.

Hurrying, the girls began to make their way to where the old diamond mine used to be. They started out on a path, but soon the path began to fade, and they found themselves deep in the woods.

Stopping, Jenny asked, "Where do we go now? These trees are so thick I can't even see the sun to tell what direction we are going."

Kate pulled a paper out of her pocket. "I made this sketch last night after talking to Grandma. If I'm right, we should go that way." Kate pointed off to the south. Jenny looked at the map Kate had drawn.

"This is pretty good," she commented.

"I looked up the park map on the internet last night and sketched it. Then I went and added in the information Grandma Jo told me. We shouldn't be too far from where the old factory used to be."

"All I know is your map sure beats mine. That was smart to do the extra sketches."

Kate informed her, "Do you know that when the mining company was first opened up, they were mining and finding several diamonds daily, but then the supply seemed to dwindle. That's when the owners finally figured out that some of the men working there were stealing from them, and they started hiring men to patrol the factory from the ceiling. So they were guarding from the rafters even before Hans was there.

"Evidently, once they had the armed guards stationed up in the rafters walking back and forth, no worker was going to chance stealing a diamond, so the factory suddenly began producing more of the valuable stones."

The girls began to see a clearing ahead. "Over there, that has to be where we want to go," said Kate. As they began to near the clearing, all of a sudden Kate held out her arm forcefully to stop Jenny from taking another step. "Shhhh . . . ," she said in a dramatic whisper. "Look!"

Jenny carefully lifted her head to peek over the top of the waist-high brush. About a hundred yards away, she could see scattered lumber and timber. It did look like an old building had been torn down.

Creeping around the edge of the clearing on the far side from the girls was Whiskers. With his grizzled features, white bushy hair, and skunk-striped beard, he looked even more frightening to Jenny now that she was seeing him from a shorter distance.

"Look at him," whispered Kate. "It looks like his pack has those swimming pool noodles on it to cushion it."

Jenny nodded. "We've seen him several times around the park. He always has that long carved walking stick. That may be part of his way of protecting himself from the wildlife in the woods."

Whiskers paused and looked around, eyeing the trees and scanning the woods.

"Duck!" whispered Jenny. Both girls ducked down behind the thickets of grass with the protection of a cluster of trees. After waiting quietly for a few moments, Kate peeked out.

"He looks like he's moving on away from us," said Kate.

"Dad thinks Whiskers leaves the plowed field every day, but I wonder if he lives in the woods." Jenny gave a shiver. "Do you think it's safe for us to go out and look around? Are you sure he's gone?"

This time, Kate stood up and looked at the old mine remains. "Seriously, he is gone, so let's go poke around some."

Jenny admired Kate's fearlessness. "Okay, let's go," she said as she pushed the brush aside and stepped on into the clearing.

11

At first, the girls kept looking over their shoulders to make sure they weren't being watched by Whiskers. But once they realized there was no flash of pink from the pool noodles, they let their curiosity at exploring the old diamond mining company take over and threw caution to the wind.

"This looks like it might have been the corner of the building," said Kate. "Why don't we start here and see if we can walk around the perimeter of where the building used to be. We've first got to find where the building actually stood."

"Sounds like a good idea." The girls began at the corner they could see. The building had obviously been torn apart, probably so the lumber from it could be used for another structure. They began walking slowly, carefully looking at the ground, trying to determine where the wall of the building had been.

"Here," said Jenny. "I think this might be where the side of the building was. See how if you stand and look down this way that there is sort of an invisible straight line? I bet that's where this wall sat. More than likely when they were tearing the building apart, they scattered the materials to the right and left. And since it was abandoned after that, you can tell by the debris of the destruction where the clean line is that would represent the wall."

Kate scanned her eyes down the line that Jenny was referring to. She was silent for a moment before speaking up. "I think you are right. You can tell that there is a sort of line. Good eye, Jenny! Let's walk it and see if we can find where the turn is in the building and where our next invisible line will be for the next wall."

For the next hour, the two girls paced the perimeter of where the old mining building used to stand. After the first corner, they realized they would need to mark them, so they wouldn't have to look for them again the next time they were there.

"Here, let's use some of the stones to pile at the corners," said Jenny.

"I'm not sure that's a good idea. We don't know if that old guy—"

"Whiskers," interjected Jenny. "That's what we call him."

"What if Whiskers is looking for the same thing? We don't know if he's heard about the legend of the German diamond. Let's figure out some other way to mark the corners where we'll know where they are, but it won't be a dead giveaway to anyone else who might be out here snooping around."

Jenny nodded her agreement, scanning the area. "I have it!" she exclaimed. "How about we use the trees that are around this open area to flag where the corners are. No one would ever guess that the trees would be related to the corners of the mining and washing company."

"I have some ribbon in my backpack," she continued. "Do you think we could just tie a bit to a low branch?" Jenny unzipped the backpack and began digging through the bottom of it. "Finally!" she said, pulling out a blue hair ribbon.

"Well, it's the best we have right now," said Kate. "Let's tie it to the tree over there. It's closest to the first corner we found. We're going to have to get out of here soon and get back to your RV. Maybe we can search one corner at a time and then move the ribbon as we finish and then start a new corner."

"Good idea," said Jenny. "If anyone sees one ribbon, they won't think much about it, but if they were to see several of them, then it might make them suspicious."

The girls carefully tied Jenny's blue ribbon near the base of a large sycamore tree. "Let's go now," said Kate as they finished. The girls took off back through the woods to get home to Jenny's trailer. As they looked back, they could only see the blue ribbon if they carefully focused.

"Our search area should be safe. We'll come back next week. If you want, you can come out by yourself to look around, but Grandma Jo only agreed for me to come out to do our 'project' on Mondays and Wednesdays." Kate glanced down at her watch. "We don't want to be late for her to pick me up, especially on this first visit."

Jenny nodded her agreement. "Let's go! I may come back out tomorrow to look around on my own. If I can do that, we'll save even more time when we are looking together."

Getting back to the campsite was easier than it had been finding the old mining company. The girls were already getting familiar with the trail. They entered the clearing near the Shoemaker's RV. "Here we are, home at last!" cried Jenny.

Kate stopped abruptly at the door of the RV. She whirled around and faced Jenny. "I didn't even think about getting rocks," said Kate. "If Grandma asks, I'll just tell her that we were scoping out the area today to see where we want to search. We'll have to remember to bring a bag to collect some rock samples next time, so if either your dad or Grandma Jo ask, we can show them our work."

"Good idea," Jenny said. "I'll get some gathered that we can keep here." As the girls stored the tools in the RV, they heard Grandma Jo's car pull into the campsite.

"Hi, Grandma Jo," called Jenny.

"Hi, Jenny," replied Grandma Jo. She looked at Kate. "Did you girls have any luck with your search for the project?'

"Oh, yes," replied Jenny, smiling. "It seemed like we found something at every corner."

12

A week later, Jenny decided to not ride the bus home. She still hadn't gotten quite used to being alone and dreaded going home when Kate wouldn't be with her. She still kept the truck key with her around her neck on a chain, so she had the option of waiting for her dad.

Jenny headed to the mill. She and Kate had been working hard on the days they could to search for the German diamond. Zack had been so curious about Kate riding the bus that they finally had to let him in on the secret since he knew Mrs. Lancaster hadn't assigned a science project. To keep him sworn to secrecy, the girls had promised to let him search for the diamond with them. But, they told him, if he breathed a word of what they were doing to anyone, the deal would be off.

Jenny decided to walk to the grocery store to get a snack. Now that Dad was working overtime at the mill, he had a little cash to spare, and he'd told her he'd keep a small stash for her under the floor mat of the truck, so she could always have access to some money if she needed it. Tonight, they were going to cook hot dogs over the campfire, so she needed to get some hot dog buns. After getting the money from under the floor mat, Jenny walked on into town. The bell on the door jingled as Jenny entered Rattlers One Stop Shop. Hearing the bell, Mr. Grimes raised his head. When he saw Jenny, he quickly pasted a smile on his face.

"Oh, hi, Jenny!" he greeted her warmly. "How are things going these days? I haven't seen you around as much."

Jenny groaned inwardly. "I'm fine, Mr. Grimes. Sometimes I ride the bus home. That's why you haven't seen me in here as much."

"Really? I'm surprised your dad lets you go home to the park alone. You do still live at the state park, don't you?"

His interrogation was starting to make her nervous. "I'm not alone. I have friends who live by me."

"I know I wouldn't let Tim stay by himself out there. It's too lonely now that the campers are gone. So, what do you do after school when you're there? Have any adventures you want to talk about?"

Jenny was sure now that he was on a fishing expedition to see if he could find out if she was searching for the diamond. She shrugged, not wanting to give away any information. "No, no adventures. Life is as boring as always." She moved away from the counter and went over to the aisle with the hot dog buns.

"You know, with you being new to town, I don't know if anyone has ever talked to you about all of the legends around here about diamonds. That's all they are, just legends. People do find stones out at the mining field where it is plowed, but the stories about these large diamonds aren't true. I hope you're not wasting your time trying to search for anything, like the lost German diamond."

By now, Jenny wanted nothing more to do than get out of the store! She didn't want to answer any of his questions. Plus, she didn't like how Mr. Grimes kept stressing that she was alone out at the park. She was afraid anything she said might give Mr. Grimes more information than he and Tim already had with the word list.

Jenny nodded, showing her agreement. "I know. My friend, Kate, told me that there were lots of legends around town. I'm not trying to find anything." With that comment she plopped down the money to pay for her snack and hot dog buns and ran out the door.

"Hey, you've got some change coming!" Jenny didn't look back. "No problem," said Mr. Grimes under his breath. "You'll be back at some point. And I'm sure you'll start talking about what you are up to . . . or I'll find out for myself what you're doing at the park."

13

Monday at lunch, Kate and Zack pulled up chairs beside Jenny in the cafeteria. "We're on for today, right?" asked Kate.

Jenny nodded as she swallowed the bite of her ham sandwich. The cafeteria ladies had put too much mayonnaise on it, and she wiped her mouth with a napkin. "Yes, today we need to get out and search. I had to go into the grocery store again, and Tim's dad kept grilling me. He keeps telling me how alone I am out there. It kind of feels like he thinks something bad is going to happen to me.

"While Dad was working on the truck on Saturday, I poked around the park a little. There were a lot of tourists around, but I think I saw Tim across the way in the woods not far from the plowed field. I ducked behind some trees and headed to the visitor center. If it was

Tim, I didn't want him to know I saw him. I'm worried they are going to search and find the diamond out there."

Zack turned and looked across the lunchroom to where Tim was sitting with his buddies at a long rectangular table. "He seems to be acting normal, at least as normal as Tim knows how to act!" Zack added with a grin.

Kate spoke up, "As soon as we get off the bus, we need to get to Jenny's trailer, drop our things, and then get started. We've searched three of the corners of the old mine. Once we finish with the fourth one today, I don't know where we'll look next if we don't find anything!"

Talking with heads huddled, they didn't notice when Tim approached. "So, what's so important that you are talking about?" he sneered. "Found any diamonds yet?"

Kate jerked up her head and looked Tim square in the eye. "Bug off, Tim Grimes, you don't know anything!"

With his brow furrowed, he hissed back, "Yes, I do. My dad and I were out at the crater over the weekend, and we know where you're hunting." He paused. "We found a blue hair ribbon. And we can tell what you are thinking from that word list you gave me."

"Gave you?" This time, it was Jenny who spoke up and her voice started to rise. "Gave you?" she repeated, almost shouting by now.

"We didn't GIVE you that list, you STOLE it from us!"

"Whoa, what's going on over here?" Mrs. Lancaster rushed over from the teachers' dining table.

Tim took a step back. "Nothing," he said, raising both hands in surrender. "I don't know what she's so upset about. It's nothing, right, Kate?" He gave Kate a pointed look.

Kate understood. The last thing they needed was for someone else to know about the word list and their search for the diamond. "Really, Mrs. Lancaster," said Kate. "It isn't anything. Tim had just said something earlier to Jenny, and he was apologizing, and she wasn't quite ready to accept his apology."

Kate looked over at Jenny, nodding at her, hoping she'd play along. Taking a deep breath to calm herself, Jenny said, "That's right, Mrs. Lancaster, we're fine." Then she looked at Tim. "Thanks for the apology."

"You're welcome." Tim grinned wickedly and walked off.

Mrs. Lancaster left with a backward glance over her shoulder to make sure no one followed Tim out of the lunchroom. The three reconvened with their huddle.

"The nerve of the guy! He admitted he and his dad are searching as well. If they find the diamond first, we'll never get to stay here. I'll have to move again!" Jenny was near tears. She hadn't realized how much she was counting on the diamond to be her ticket to a normal life in this pretty little town. She knew the proverbial clock was ticking, not only for finding the diamond before Tim and his dad, but also to find the diamond before the weather started changing for fall and her dad felt like they'd have to move because their trailer would be too cold.

"The bell's about to ring," said Zack. "We can finish up our plan on the bus, but for now we need to head back to class and just act normal. We need to not let on to Tim about our plan to go search today. His dad usually runs the store during the weekday hours, and then he has another manager who runs it in the evenings until they close and on the weekend. It's doubtful they'll try to search again before next weekend, so that gives us this week to have our final search."

The afternoon moved as slow as molasses. Jenny lost count of the number of times she looked up at the clock on the wall above Mrs. Lancaster's desk. Normally she enjoyed Mrs. Lancaster's lessons, but today she just couldn't focus. All she could think about was the great friends she'd made and how Murfreesboro had become home to her. Zack and Kate were the best, no only, friends she'd ever really had. And the rest of the class had been pretty nice to her, too. Tim was her only real problem, and if they found the diamond, surely he'd leave her alone again. She really wanted to keep living here and found herself thinking about the Garrison house.

One day after she'd left Grandma Jo's, Jenny had walked to the Garrison house on her way to the mill. The house was small and kind of looked like Grandma Jo's house. It was definitely an older home, but that didn't bother Jenny. After living in a beat up RV, this place was as beautiful to her as a brand new home featured in a magazine. The Garrison house had a porch that reached across the front of the house, and there was a weathered porch swing hanging at one end.

It looked as if the previous renters had moved out. The grass was getting high from not being cut, and the shrubs were tall, almost reaching the top of the porch wall. Looking up and down the street carefully, and not seeing anyone out, Jenny had scooted up on the porch and pressed her face to the front windows. The window to the left of the front door looked like it was the living room window. The room was a nondescript square, but there were wood floors and an opening to the back that looked like it would hold a dining room table. *Wow, wouldn't it be cool to be able to sit at a table to eat instead of having a table that had to be folded up every night into a bed?* She had walked over to the other window and peered inside. This was probably a bedroom window. It looked like the room had a closet on the side, and there was another window on another wall. *What would it be like to have an entire room this size to call your own?* And there was more than likely another bedroom as well, so Dad could have his own space.

Still keeping an eye out to see if anyone was watching her and seeing no one, she walked over to the swing and sat down. It gave slightly with her weight, but once she realized it would hold her, she relaxed and gently nudged the porch floor with her tennis shoe and let the swing rock her. Closing her eyes, she imagined that this house belonged to them.

Jenny knew she was setting herself up for heartbreak with her dream of staying. Even though she knew it was a long shot, she was determined to give the search for the German diamond all her effort and energy.

14

The next afternoon, the trio talked as they made their way down the trail. "I can't believe we're down to our last corner to search," said Jenny. "The diamond just has to be there, and we've got to find it today."

"We've searched everywhere that it could possibly be around the old building, so it's got to be at this last corner. We're going to have to make sure that we are super careful today as we sift through the soil," said Kate. "Zack, why don't you do the first round of sifting with the large screen, and then I'll sort through the fine screen. Jenny, you can shovel the soil for us. I know you were looking on our last visit through the screens, but since I've had the most experience, let me do it today since it's the last try."

The children were so intent on their systematic search of the corner of the old diamond mine, they were unaware they were being watched until they heard the snap of a branch.

Jenny whirled around with her shovel and gave a little scream. Zack and Kate raised their heads from sifting as if on cue.

Whiskers came striding out of the woods, shaking his fist at them. Spit flew from his mouth, and his eyes looked electric. "What are you kids doing here? Get away! It isn't safe for you to be here. This is private property!"

Kate swiveled her head back and forth between Jenny and Zack. They were frozen in place.

"Go!" screamed Whiskers again. "Go! And don't let me see you here again!"

Turning his head, he looked Jenny square in the eye. "You, little missy, need to watch your step out here in these woods all by yourself."

At last, the three broke free and took off running down the path back to the RV campsite. Jenny still clutched the shovel; Zack and Kate each had a screen in hand. They didn't stop running or say a word until they were safely inside Jenny's RV.

Jenny spoke first, "That scared me to death the way he kept screaming at us!"

"And I don't know why he kept telling us that what we were doing was dangerous. There's no danger out here that I've heard of," added Zack.

Kate nodded. "I agree! I thought he was going crazy. Jenny, did you ask your dad about him? I'm starting to think he does camp out here in the woods. Maybe he thinks this old torn down place is his."

Zack spoke up, "Or maybe he had family who lived out here. There was once a town called Kimberling right near the part of the park where we've been searching. It was a town that was built to house all the people who came to work at the mines. Once the mines went out of business and closed their doors, the town was torn down, and it went back to being farmland."

"That's weird," said Jenny. "I don't think I've ever heard of a town being torn down before."

Zack continued, "I asked my granddad about it last night and tried not to let on why I was so interested in everything out here. Anyway, Granddad told me about where the town once was." He looked at Jenny. "You know where the Mauney House is?" She nodded. "It's basically that whole area across the road from it. People lived there and could literally walk to their job at the mines."

Kate's voice got soft. "Jenny, we can maybe try to search one last time. I know Grandma thinks we're wrapping up our project. And, with the way Whiskers acted today, I think we need to wrap up the search soon."

Even though she didn't want to agree with Kate, Jenny nodded her head. "Please, guys, let's try that one last corner."

Zack and Kate exchanged a look, then Kate said, "Yes, Jenny, we'll search the last corner."

15

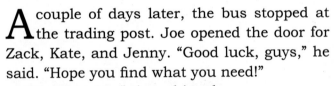

A couple of days later, the bus stopped at the trading post. Joe opened the door for Zack, Kate, and Jenny. "Good luck, guys," he said. "Hope you find what you need!"

"Thanks, Joe," they chimed.

With the exception of Whiskers, the trail was no longer scary to Jenny. Even on the days when Kate and Zack weren't with her, she easily walked by herself. There had been a time when the leafless vines swinging from the trees frightened her and made her think there were snakes perched on every branch. Now she didn't even look up into the trees and worry about what was above her.

Unlocking the door to the trailer, Jenny let Zack and Kate in. She'd quit worrying about what they thought of her home. She knew they accepted her as their friend and didn't judge her on where she lived. It was such a relief to be able to relax and be herself without worrying how they would think of her.

Grabbing their digging tools and a thermos of water, Zack pulled a bag of crackers out of his backpack. "I brought a snack for us today," he said. Without Jenny having mentioned anything about the family budget, the other two had filled in with bringing snacks to share from their homes. It was an unspoken agreement that neither Zack nor Kate made Jenny wonder if she was pulling her weight with the group. To make her feel better, they reminded her that she was providing the meeting place and digging tools. Dad had gotten the tools when they moved to the park.

They gathered up their supplies and headed to their work on the fourth and final corner of the old mine. "I hope we can search without Whiskers showing up," said Jenny. "Hopefully he's in another part of the park. I haven't seen him around again, so I didn't tell Dad about what had happened." Jenny knew Dad would be furious if he knew what she was up to, so she thought it better to keep quiet about it.

True to their routine, the three of them settled in to work once they were at the mine site. Jenny began methodically shoveling small clumps of soil and shaking them into the tray with the large-screened openings. Zack gently shook the tray back and forth, allowing all of the fine loose soil to sift into the second fine-screened tray. The chunks that remained on the second tray were what they searched through.

Kate gently brushed the remaining soil back and forth with her fingers. She carefully analyzed any chunks of soil that seemed promising. After what felt like hours, but was only about forty-five minutes, Kate spoke up. "Seriously"—she sighed—"I don't know what else to do to find the diamond."

They were defeated. They had searched the soil at every corner of the old mine carefully. They'd sifted and sorted through buckets of soil with no luck. They had only come away with a couple pieces of quartz and some fine blisters on their hands from all of the digging.

"I agree," said Zack. "I don't have any other ideas on what to do or where to look."

"We can't give up now," Jenny begged. "We've just got to find the lost diamond." She looked pleadingly at Zack and Kate.

Kate looked at her friend, her heart going out to her. She knew that Jenny had put all of her hopes and dreams into having the lost German diamond be the ticket to staying in Murfreesboro.

"I know you don't want to give up, Jenny, but we've looked at the base of every corner of the foundation. And there are too many trees for us to dig underneath. I'd have no idea where to look there. Plus, Grandma Jo keeps asking me why we haven't finished our project yet. I'm starting to think she may be getting suspicious about what we are up to.

"Why don't we try to think of another way for you to get to stay here and not move away?"

Jenny's heart sank. She knew Kate was right. They'd exhausted their search, and the whole science project ruse needed to come to an end before Grandma Jo and her dad found out what they'd really been up to. "I understand," she said. "Who knows, maybe I'll be able to look a little longer on my own before the weather starts to get chilly." Jenny tried to make them feel better.

It was with heavy hearts that they trudged back to the RV. Zack handed the small trowel to Jenny along with a sifting tray. "I'm sorry, Jenny," he said, looking her in the eye, "that we didn't find the diamond. I know how much it meant to you."

"It's okay, Zack," Jenny replied. She didn't want him to feel bad after all the hard work he'd done to help keep her dream alive. "At least we gave it a try."

Zack gave a wave and headed across the road and down the trail to go home. Grandma Jo's car came around the bend in the road. She gave a wave to the two girls.

"I brought some brownies for you to share with your dad, Jenny." Grandma Jo handed a foil-wrapped paper plate to her. Then, turning to Kate she asked, "So, are you about to wrap up the project?"

Kate nodded. "Yes, we actually finished today. I'm going to wash the stones at our house if that is okay, and then I'll take them to school, right, Jenny?"

Jenny reached into the RV and pulled out the bag of stones and crystals they'd gathered the past few weeks of their hunt. They'd planned all along to have some rocks to prove they'd been working on the science project.

Jenny handed the bag to Kate and told Grandma Jo, "Thank you for the brownies. And thank you for letting Kate come out to the park to work with me."

"I'm glad she found such a good friend in you! I bet you girls will make an A on your project." With that, she and Kate got in the car and pulled onto State Park Road.

Her heart sinking, Jenny watched the car disappear down the road. Even though she'd still see Kate at school, she knew the odds were against her staying in Murfreesboro. Given her dad's track record, he could come home any night now with a plan to pack up and move. Jenny made up her mind. She would just have to keep looking for the diamond by herself. It was too late to do anything else tonight, but she was determined that she would go back to the mining and washing site tomorrow and start digging under the trees. After all, Hans had specifically mentioned a tree in the list of words.

16

The next morning Jenny remained in her bed when Dad knocked on the thin particle wood door to wake her up.

"Time to rise and shine, kiddo!" he called, giving his routine rat-a-tat-tat knock on the door. Jenny didn't move. When Dad didn't hear her getting up, he knocked one more time. "Come on, Jenny, you know I can't be late to work!"

"I don't feel so good," she moaned.

"Can I come in?" Dad asked.

"Sure," she replied in a weak voice.

When Dad entered Jenny's room, he took in her appearance. "Do you have a fever?" He reached over to feel her forehead.

Jenny shrugged. "I don't know. It's mainly my stomach. Maybe I ate something that upset it . . . I don't think I can go to school today."

"I've got to be at work, Jenny. I'm still the newest man there and want to make a good impression." Dad sounded concerned about the job.

Jenny was surprised. She hadn't known her dad to ever care much about any of his jobs. Maybe he was making friends, too. Still, she couldn't gamble on that. "I can stay here by myself. I'll be fine. And I promise to stay close to the RV."

"I don't know, Jenny, how I feel about you staying out here all by yourself. It's one thing when it is after school for a little bit, and I know your friends are in and out, but you'd be home all day with no way to reach me."

"Do they have a phone number where I could reach you at the mill if I kept the cell phone, Dad?" asked Jenny.

Her father paused and thought. "Well, yes, there is a phone out in the floor office. I have the number programmed in my phone. See, here's the number. If you promise that you'll stay in the RV and not go out at all, even for the restrooms, I'll let you stay. You have to use our bathroom here in the RV and give me your word about staying in."

"Trust me, Dad, I don't feel like going anywhere. I'll just stay here in bed and sleep some more. I have a book from school in my backpack, so I can read it if I feel up to doing anything."

Jenny could tell by the expression on Dad's face that he was torn. He really didn't want to leave her out here all alone. Finally, he sighed heavily. "Okay. I'll let you do it. But I'll call from the mill office at my lunch break to check on you. Then I'll see if I can get out of there a little early."

"Really, Dad, you don't need to worry. I'll be fine right here and promise I won't go anywhere."

Jenny waited until she heard the truck drive away before flinging back the covers and jumping out of bed. Today, she told herself, she'd find that German diamond. She'd have the whole day to look, and she just knew in her heart that everything would fall into place.

Quickly gathering the digging tools, she put the trowel, a bottle of water, and some snacks in her backpack. The sifting trays wouldn't fit, and she didn't have Zack or Kate to help her haul them around. She looked around her room, trying to figure how she was going to manage on her own. Then, it hit her like a brick. She could use one of her dad's belts to cinch the trays onto her backpack. That way, her hands would still be free for climbing on the narrow trails.

Surprised at her own creativity, she cinched the first belt tight. She'd actually used two belts, one to go around the backpack from side to side, the other to connect over the top and bottom. Lifting the now heavy pack on her back, she tested the weight. It was cumbersome, but she could manage it. Taking one last look around the RV to make sure she'd gotten everything, she looped the keys around her neck, tucked the cell phone into her backpack, and closed the door behind her. *Today's the day*, she thought to herself, *today's the day*. Then under her breath she said, "It just *has* to be!"

Stepping out of the RV, she paused to look around the campsite. There were no other campers nearby. There had been the occasional retired couple show up to camp during the week, but all the families who had been camping at the park were long gone once school and fall sports had begun. The water park was closed as well. Even though Jenny knew the visitors center and ranger station were only a couple of hundred yards away down the wooded path, it felt as if she were the only person around. Who knows, she thought, maybe she was. The visitor center didn't open until nine, and it was just now eight o'clock.

Taking off, she headed back in the direction of the old diamond mine site. She wasn't sure how she was going to know which tree to start with on the digging but she prayed that somehow she'd get some sort of inspiration when she got there. She pulled out her list of clues to remind her as if she didn't already know the words from memory.

"Diamond, ground, corner, base, tree, diamond . . ." Lost in thought, she mindlessly followed the trail that she and Kate and Zack had been walking day in and day out.

Entering into the clearing, she slowly walked in a circle around the perimeter of where the building had stood. Where should she start? The pack was heavy, but she didn't want to unload her tools and supplies until she was sure where she wanted to begin.

The sun had been rising in the sky, but some clouds drifted over it. Jenny looked up as the lighting changed. Giving a little shiver, she decided to try to figure out what would have been the back door of the mine. *What,* she wondered, *would Hans have been thinking when he tried to find a place to hide the diamond?* Maybe the prison guards gave the prisoners a break from their work. If there was a back door, Hans could have slipped out back to hide the diamond. Head down, she shuffled slowly around the footing. Finding what she thought might have been the back of the building, she went to where she thought the door would have been and stood for a long time, looking at the edge of the clearing. She saw a tall oak off to the right and decided to have it be her first digging spot. It was definitely an old tree, so it would have been growing here when the mine was open. She carefully unbelted the screens and got out the trowel and old towel she'd brought along to sit on as she dug. All was silent as she began to dig and sift.

After awhile, Jenny reached into her backpack and looked at the cell phone to check the time. It felt like she'd been in one spot for a couple of hours, but only an hour had passed. Just as she was debating about moving to another tree, the trowel hit something solid. Excited, Jenny began digging faster, not paying any attention to where she was throwing the dirt. After several minutes, she could see something that appeared to be metal in the ground. She brushed at the dirt with her hands, and when that didn't remove the dirt, she began using the trowel to scrape at the top of the metal. Finally, she could see edges and realized she had uncovered the top of a small metal box. It took several more minutes of tireless digging and scraping, but she finally pried it loose from the soil and pulled it out.

Only about a four-inch square, the box had a lock on it. Jenny had a shiver of excitement. This had to be the diamond! She reached for the trowel to try to dig further to see if she could find a key. That's when she felt as if she were being watched. She glanced up and was shocked to meet a pair of eyes.

"Aren't you supposed to be in school?"

17

Jenny looked up into the face of Mr. Grimes. "I, uh, I, uh, wasn't feeling too well this morning," she stammered.

Lester Grimes gave her a small cynical smile. "The police would be real interested in finding out that you are truant from school. Don't you know there are laws against missing school for no reason?"

Jenny backed up. "I'm not truant. I wasn't feeling well."

"So what do you have there, Jenny? What have you done? You know you don't have any right to be out here taking things."

Jenny looked down at the box in her hand. The metal was a dark color, having been buried for no telling how long. She felt frozen in place.

"I asked you a question, girl, what have you got there?" Grimes raised his voice. "You'd better hand it over to me, or I'm going to have to turn you into the police for stealing from the park."

Jenny backed up a couple of steps as Grimes took another step in her direction. "I wasn't stealing, I promise," said Jenny.

"Looks like it to me . . . you just wait, you're in so much trouble!"

Jenny didn't know what Grimes might try to do to her. And she didn't want him to steal the box. Turning abruptly, she ran away.

"Come back here!" he shouted. "You give me that box now!"

Jenny continued to run although she didn't know where she was. She'd taken off into the woods without a second thought as to the direction to go. She couldn't go back on the trail she knew by heart because Grimes had come in that way, and she would have had to run around him. Her heart racing, Jenny slowed her step and listened carefully. She could hear Grimes thrashing in the dense greenery. It appeared that Grimes wasn't close on her heels. She looked up and saw that the sky had gotten a darker shade of gray than it had when she encountered Grimes, and it was starting to look like rain. Where in the world was she? She felt hopelessly lost in a jungle of green.

"Jenny, where are you? Get out here now!" She heard Grimes' voice again, shouting.

Jenny crouched as still as she could in some underbrush.

"Jenny!"

Grimes' voice sounded like it was maybe getting farther away. She could hear him still thrashing and beating the thicket. It seemed as if she might be in the opposite direction of where he was searching based on how his voice sounded.

Down, she thought, *I have to get down this mountain.* Trying to stay out of Grimes' sight, she ran frantically as fast as she could, her arms and legs getting scraped by the branches. Panting, she grabbed a tree to catch her breath. Looking around, she tried to get her bearings and realized she was lost. She had no idea where she was! Listening carefully, she tried to see if she could still hear Grimes, but there appeared to be no sight or sound of him.

The first of several large raindrops began to fall from the sky. Jenny looked up again at the darkening sky. As the rain started to fall, she knew she was going to have to do something. She was hopelessly lost, and in her hurry to run away from Grimes, she'd left her backpack with the phone in it up at the mining site.

Moving now at a slower pace, she pushed her way on down the mountain. She clutched the small metal box in one hand and used the other hand to balance as she went. At times, it was hazardous because the ground was getting slippery in places from the rain.

Lightning streaked across the sky and then the rain began to pound. *I've got to find shelter*, thought Jenny. *I can't be out here in the middle of these tall trees with all the lightning.* She slowed down her pace, carefully working her way down the mountain. It was treacherous as she slipped and slid. At one point, she started to fall. It was only by grabbing one of the snake-like vines that grew in the park that she kept from sliding and slamming her head into a tree.

Tears began to course down her cheeks. She wasn't sure how she was going to get somewhere safe. It had been some time since she'd seen or heard Grimes, and the rain was still coming down in sheets. That's when she saw it—the Mauney House looming across the road. She'd ended up on the far side of the park in the farming field that used to be the city of Kimberling. Once she crossed the highway bridge over Prairie Creek, she could run up the drive of the house.

Breaking into the clearing, she gave up on the thought of trying to hide from Grimes. Worried about the lightning that was streaking across the sky, she dashed across the open field; her hair dripping and feet flying.

As she got closer to the Mauney House, she hesitated, thinking of all the stories she'd heard about how it had been abandoned and was haunted. Fearing the storm now more than the house itself, Jenny looked around to see if Grimes was in sight as she made her way up the steep drive. Water was washing down the gravel, covering her tennis shoes. Her feet were soaking wet.

She stepped onto the porch. If only she could find shelter here without trying to go inside. She really didn't want to go in after hearing that the house was haunted, but as the storm continued to intensify, she was fearful of being struck by lightning. Plus, she was soaked to the skin. Working her way around to the back of the house, she searched for some way to get inside. She wanted to stay away from the front of the house where she might be seen from the road in case Grimes was now in his car searching for her.

There was a door on her left as she crept around the corner of the covered porch. Still clutching the metal box, her fingers seemingly frozen to it, she reached for the hammered iron door handle. *Gee, this is old*, she thought. She'd never seen a handle like this. Turning it slowly, the knob turned, and she gave a sigh of relief. It was unlocked, what luck!

18

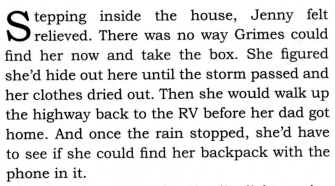

Stepping inside the house, Jenny felt relieved. There was no way Grimes could find her now and take the box. She figured she'd hide out here until the storm passed and her clothes dried out. Then she would walk up the highway back to the RV before her dad got home. And once the rain stopped, she'd have to see if she could find her backpack with the phone in it.

As her eyes adjusted to the dim light coming in from the windows, she saw the wall murals that Kate had talked about on the bus that day. Strobes of lightning illuminated the full-sized paintings on each of the walls. This was really cool. She was so taken by surprise at the murals that she almost forgot about her dripping hair and soaked clothes.

She moved on around the room to explore. In the dim light, she began to notice that someone must have been there more recently because she noticed a camp stool in the corner and an aged army blanket beside it. All of a sudden, her heart lurched as she heard a voice.

"What are you doing here, girl?" The tone was gruff, but it wasn't Lester Grimes' voice.

Jenny whirled around and found herself face to face with Whiskers. She jumped back. "I'm sorry. I was just trying to get in from the rain." She looked about wildly, trying to see how she could escape. All of a sudden, the fear she'd been dealing with being pursued by Lester Grimes got the best of her. "I'm scared!" she burst out. "That awful Mr. Grimes has been chasing me in the Crater of Diamonds Park! And now you are here! You aren't going to hurt me, are you?" Fear was etched across her face.

The gruff exterior on Whiskers' wrinkle-creased face was quickly replaced by a look of concern. "Why in the world is Grimes chasing you?"

Jenny continued to sob. "It's because of this," she admitted, holding up the box. "I found it this morning, and he saw me take it out of the ground. He told me I'd stolen it and had to give it to him. He said I was stealing something that wasn't mine." Her shoulders heaved. "All I want to do is get to stay here to live in Murfreesboro!"

By now, Jenny was a basket of emotions. Whiskers looked at her with his grizzled features showing concern. "Hey, there. Calm down, okay? We need to get in touch with your Dad. He's at the mill, right?"

Jenny nodded, looking up astonished. "How did you know?" she asked.

"He and I've visited once recently in the park. We're kind of kindred spirits. We're both travelers at heart, never wanting to settle down."

Jenny couldn't mask her surprise. *Whiskers had met Dad?*

"He told me a little bit about the two of you and how you'd been on the move for so many years.

"I do have a cell phone. Let me call the mill and have them get your dad to the phone. I want to get you delivered to him safely, but I don't have a car."

"What about Grimes, what if he comes down here?"

"Ah, don't worry about him right now. You'll be safe here with me. Later your dad can let the police know how he was terrorizing you up at the crater. Everyone in town knows he's up to no good. You'll be safe here with me, so don't worry." She listened while Whiskers called the sawmill.

He dialed the mill office number and talked to the foreman. After turning off his cell phone, Whiskers turned to Jenny. "They are going to give the information to your dad. I suspect he'll be headed this way as soon as he can. I told them to have him come here to the Mauney House.

"Girl, you're shaking and shivering to death!" Jenny was shaking like a leaf. And she didn't know if she was shaking totally from the cold or also from being in the same room as Whiskers and talking to him.

"I'm so cold from getting wet!"

"Here," said Whiskers. He tossed her the folded, worn army blanket. Jenny gratefully wrapped it around her shoulders. "I've never tried to light a fire in the fireplace," he admitted. "I didn't want to draw attention to the fact I was hiding out here by having smoke coming out the chimney of the house."

The warm blanket was beginning to help Jenny a little. "You live here? Is this your home?"

Whiskers took in Jenny's appearance. "Here, you can sit over here on my stool while we wait for your dad."

"I'd just as soon sit on the floor, if it's okay with you. This blanket feels so good." Jenny gave a small sneeze.

"You may have gotten yourself a cold after running all that way in the rain." Once he was certain that Jenny was settled, Whiskers slowly began to tell his story.

"You see, I lived here in Murfreesboro when I was growing up and then went off to fight in the Vietnam War. My experiences were pretty bad over there. When I came back to Arkansas, it was hard to live like a regular person. I tried but could never seem to find the right job, and my parents had both passed away.

"The one thing I remembered that I loved doing while growing up was mining for diamonds. Since I had no friends, I started going out to the park every day to mine.

"I never got a job anywhere and just kept looking for diamonds. I've been doing it for years. Some days I find little stones that I can take into town to the jeweler to sell. Other days I don't find anything, but I can at least get out into the fresh air and exercise instead of being in some small office or workspace trying to make a few bucks. I live here and there, often camping in the woods."

"I didn't know you'd met my dad," said Jenny. "When did that happen?"

"Oh, I don't know when exactly. Since you all are living at the park, I kept seeing your dad around the area. We finally struck up a conversation one day."

"I don't get it," interrupted Jenny. "I don't know why he didn't tell me about you."

"Maybe you were too busy trying to search in the park to pay attention to anything else. You and your friends were out there almost every day."

"Only two days a week," interjected Jenny.

"Two days, three days, whatever." Whiskers voice grew louder. "What in the world was so important for you three kids to be out there alone? I tried to scare you off. A public park the size of the Crater Park is no place for three kids to be out in alone!" Jenny's chin lowered. She was starting to feel ashamed. She'd been so focused on her own plan she hadn't even seen that her dad was starting to reach out and befriend others.

"What were you kids looking for? It was dangerous how you were searching around the torn down mine and washing company location. There are all sorts of rusted nails and broken glass there. It's like one huge accident waiting to happen. That's why I yelled at the three of you that day. I was trying to scare you off before someone got hurt."

"You did scare us, but we couldn't give up our search. It was too important."

"Well, you haven't answered my question. What were you looking for?"

19

Suddenly there was a loud rap on the door. The rain was still coming down, and Whiskers opened the back door, and there stood Jenny's dad. He did not look happy to see her.

"What in tarnation are you doing here, Jenny?" His voice began to rise. "Were you just pulling my leg this morning so you could look for some diamonds? You know better than to pull a stunt like that!"

"I'm sorry, Dad," began Jenny. "It's just that we've been trying so long to find the German diamond with no luck, and I had to find it, just had to! I decided to skip school today, so I could search on my own since Zack and Kate couldn't come anymore after school."

"You mean to tell me, young lady, that you three have been searching for some diamond that is nothing more than a legend? A German diamond?" Dad looked at Jenny. "What about the science project? Was that a real assignment?"

Jenny didn't say a word but slowly shook her head. Disappointment and frustration raced across Dad's face. He turned to Whiskers. "Thanks, Carl, for rescuing her and getting ahold of me. I don't know what in the world she was thinking, but she won't be thinking of diamonds in the near future because she is going to be grounded!"

"Achoo!" Jenny sneezed. "Dad," she said, "Now I really don't feel too good. Can you take me home, please? I just want to go to bed."

"Make sure she tells you about Grimes," said Whiskers. "He spotted her taking out that box she's got there and chased her down the mountain. That's how she ended up here. She'll have to tell you the whole story."

With a quick nod of farewell to Whiskers, Dad helped Jenny get to the truck. Climbing inside by him was a relief. For all the times she'd been frustrated by the way they lived and how many times they'd moved, she'd known her dad loved her. He didn't tell her often, but today, his actions spoke louder than words.

"Dad," she began.

Dad looked over at her briefly and then turned his eyes back to the road since it was still slippery outside, and the rain was still falling even though it was slowing some.

He interrupted her. "My boss told me I could take the rest of the afternoon off, so it's going to be you and me, kid, and you are going to tell me everything, and I mean *everything* that you and your friend Kate have been up to."

Jenny began to relay the story of the diamond, going back to that first visit with Grandma Jo and the cookies. To his credit, Dad listened carefully without jumping in and trying to judge her actions before she'd finished the story. For now, he wanted to understand what Jenny had done.

"And that's all there was to it, Dad," Jenny finished. "I promise. We really did try to stay safe."

"Jenny, I thought I'd taught you to be smarter than this. You and Zack and Kate could have been seriously hurt on one of your trips out to the mining company site. That place is a pure danger zone waiting for someone to get tetanus or a bad cut. I'm not happy about Grimes chasing you. I'll pay him a little visit at his store later on. And I'll make sure the park rangers and police know what he's done.

"But here's the most important thing. I need you to promise, and this time I mean really promise to give up trying to find that German diamond. I guarantee you that someone has already found it, or it has been buried so well that it will never be found, or it wasn't buried well enough, and it washed into Prairie Creek. It *is* no more!"

Jenny could tell how frustrated, scared, and angry her dad was with her.

"But look," she said, bringing out the metal box. "I did find this today, and that is why Grimes started chasing me. He figured I'd found the diamond."

Dad fingered the metal box. "I wonder what it is?" Then his voice turned quiet. "You could have been seriously hurt or killed out there on that mountain and . . ." Dad paused. "I don't know what I'd do without you, Jenny. You know you are my whole world."

Jenny nodded her understanding, her bottom lip quivering. Her mother had died giving birth to her, and somehow her dad had managed to raise her by himself. At first, he'd gone into a depression over the death of Jenny's mom. Finally he snapped out of it, realizing he was going to lose Jenny to foster care if he didn't start doing the right thing by her. As soon as he could sell the house they lived in so he could erase the memories of Jenny's mom, they'd taken off and lived in different places. At first they'd rented houses, but once her dad found the old RV, they just lived in it. That's when Jenny really started hating their way of life. It was too easy to pick up and move on when life didn't go the right way. And she was no longer a toddler who only cared about being with her one parent and having a handful of toys.

"I know, Dad, and I am sorry," Jenny began. "I guess I lost my head since I wanted to keep living here in Murfreesboro. I've made such great friends for the first time in my life, and the town is so pretty and the people are nice. That is, except for Tim and his dad! I was only trying to help us somehow get to stay here." They were silent for a moment.

"Can we try to open it, Dad?" Jenny asked softly. For a minute Dad had forgotten he was holding the box.

"You really think this could have the diamond in it?" Even Dad had a glint of hope in his eye.

Jenny nodded. "We think from the clues I told you about that Hans hid the diamond up at the mine when he found it. We searched every corner, and when we were done, I knew I had to still try to search the trees since we hadn't found anything." She looked up. "Open it, Dad, open it!"

Reaching below the miniature sink where he kept his tools, Dad pulled out a screwdriver. "Maybe I can pry it open with this."

Jenny sat breathlessly, watching every move he made. Carefully inserting the end of the screwdriver into the locked box, he began to try to turn the screwdriver so he could work the lid loose. The box was so old he figured it wouldn't be hard to get the hinges to give.

"There, Dad, there!" Jenny shouted. "It's starting to give!"

With a crack, the lid gave. "I can open it Jenny, but I think you should do the honors," said Dad. "Let's see what you found!" Hope laced Dad's voice. "Let's have a look at this German diamond."

Jenny couldn't believe it. This was the moment she'd been dreaming of and waiting for since she'd first heard the story of Lucy Newberry and Hans. She carefully took the box from her dad. Meeting his eyes, she began to lift the lid slowly. Looking inside, she felt her stomach churning. Then everything was quiet.

Dad's eyes met hers. "I'm sorry, Jenny."

Jenny wanted to scream and throw the box across the inside of the cramped trailer. The box held an arrowhead, a metal whistle, and a cat's eye marble.

There was no diamond.

"I was so sure this was it, Dad." Jenny began to cry anew. "I knew that if I found the diamond, we'd have a forever home."

"Jenny, that's enough! You actually had *my* hopes up for a minute, but this has to be over. You gave the search your best shot, but it's finished. All those hours searching and the danger you've put yourself in were just for some child's keepsakes. They were probably put there by some boys who lived in Kimberling."

"I promise I'll quit looking, Dad. I'm sorry." Tears began to trickle down Jenny's face. "I just like it here so much!"

"I like it here too, but I can't promise that we can stay. It can get pretty cold in the winter, and you know our RV doesn't heat up well. I've been able to get a little extra cash laid by but not enough for us to move into a house. For now, living in the RV is our only option." Looking around at the worn and weathered travel trailer, he added, "It's not so horrible, is it honey? It is home."

"Yes," she replied, snuffling. "It is home."

Breaking the silence, he said, "Here." He reached for the box. "Give me that, and let's get you over to the showers. I'll sit guard outside under the shelter, so you can take a long hot shower, and then we've got to get you dried off and resting."

Jenny sneezed again. "And tomorrow, young lady, you'd better be ready to go back to school!"

Jenny felt better after cleaning up and surprised herself by falling fast asleep once she lay down on her bed. She thought she might take a little nap, but she ended up sleeping for three hours. When she woke up, thinking about the day, she knew she needed to give up the quest for the diamond, but in her heart she didn't know if she could do it.

20

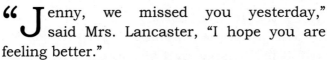

"Jenny, we missed you yesterday," said Mrs. Lancaster, "I hope you are feeling better."

Jenny nodded to her teacher. Kate and Zack looked at her curiously, trying to read her expression. "Later," mouthed Jenny. Kate gave her a little nod while she went to her seat. She'd only been seated for five minutes when she started coughing vigorously.

"Jenny, go get a drink. See if that will help," said Mrs. Lancaster.

"I'm sorry. I was out in the rain yesterday and seemed to catch a cold."

At her comment, Tim Grimes grinned at her. As she walked by, he muttered, "Out in the rain, huh?"

Jenny chose to ignore him. Getting back to class, she did her best to concentrate on the lesson. She willed the clock to move faster, wanting it to be lunchtime, so she could tell Kate and Zack about what had happened yesterday. She'd tucked the metal box full of treasures into her backpack, so she could show it to them. At least they would have something to show after all of those afternoons of digging!

"Class, pull out your reading notebooks and gather up here on the carpet for our lesson." Mrs. Lancaster kept a close eye on the class as they gathered. "Tim, I'm serious. Get your notebook and quit playing around." Tim finally quit goofing off and joined the rest of the students.

Jenny got her materials quickly, so she could find a spot by Kate on the carpet. She kept a close eye on Tim to make sure he wasn't going to end up near her. He typically sat at the back of the group, so he could mess around with his pencil and flick little wads of paper at unsuspecting classmates. And the last thing she needed today was him poking her with his pencil while she tried to pay attention to the lesson. She could tell by his comment earlier that he knew about her run-in with his dad at the state park. What amazed her is that he thought it was funny. As Jenny had thought about her race through the park and making her way in a rush down the mountain, she was thankful she hadn't been seriously hurt!

Mrs. Lancaster started the lesson, bringing Jenny out of her thoughts. "Yesterday I read the story by Eve Bunting titled *So Far From the Sea*. The story was about a Japanese prisoner of war camp in Eastern California. Remember, we talked about the bombing of Pearl Harbor and how even though there were thousands of Japanese Americans living on United States soil, they were considered possible traitors once the United States declared war on Japan. Our book, *So Far From the Sea*, took us back and forth in time, letting us see the memorial of the prisoner of war camp and then back to when the family was arriving there.

"Today, we are reading another story about the Japanese prisoner of war camps, but it is told differently. In the book we are reading today, the author takes us to a different camp. But this author, Ken Mochizuki, tells of how the people living in the camp went about trying to survive mentally. After being free citizens, it would have been very difficult to be a prisoner and having every move you made monitored from armed guards.

"You have to imagine how different their lives would have been in the camp. Men and women who had been working at jobs would be at loose ends. Children wouldn't have had their regular schools to attend. It would have been very difficult."

Zack raised his hand. "I just don't get it, Mrs. Lancaster, why did they lock them up if they hadn't done anything wrong?"

Mrs. Lancaster nodded. "I agree, Zack, it seems so wrong doesn't it? In a way it was another form of discrimination." She turned back to address the entire class. "What I want you to do today is listen to this second story, *Baseball Saved Us*, and make notes comparing the two books."

As Mrs. Lancaster read of the hardships of the prisoners, she commented, "It would have been so hard to have to sit with nothing to do. When the main character's brother smarts off to his dad, the father can tell that they must get something to focus on to help them not feel so helpless. Listen as I read this part about how the Japanese prisoners of war struggled to create the baseball field.

Ben raised his hand. "That would have been hard to have made an entire baseball diamond without any equipment."

"Yeah," agreed Zack. "I watched them when they were putting in the baseball practice diamonds up across town. I'd ride my bike over there in the evening. I really liked watching them make the dugout and tape off the field carefully."

Jenny was listening to the conversation when she felt a jab in her ribs. She glanced with surprise at Kate, who pointed to her reading notebook. She'd written a note lightly with pencil in the margin: "The baseball fields we use in town are where the prisoner of war camp used to be." Jenny absorbed this piece of information. She looked at Kate with a question in her eyes. Kate gave her head a little shake and mouthed, "Later."

Mrs. Lancaster continued with the lesson, and Jenny tried to focus, but it was impossible. Her mind began to race, and she started mentally saying Hans' clue words in her head: diamond, ground, corner, base, tree, diamond. Could it be possible? Could they have been searching in the wrong place all this time? Jenny thought she just might wiggle right off the carpet!

21

Kate could hardly contain herself. Waiting until Zack and Jenny had pulled up their seats, she motioned for them to lean in. "Did you think what I was thinking during the reading lesson this morning?"

"Yes!" said Jenny. "I couldn't help but picture Hans and the other prisoners making a baseball diamond and playing the game to pass time when they weren't assigned to do their other work."

"Diamond, ground, corner, base, tree, diamond," said Zack. "The words all fit for baseball! And the prisoner of war camp was located exactly where we have our baseball field for the town league today. It would have been the exact one that Hans built and the other prisoners would have played on."

"Let's go to my house right after school and tell Grandma Jo what we've discovered. Zack, is there any way you could somehow come home with me, too, so you can go with us to the park?"

"What park?" Tim appeared behind Jenny. "Now what are you all cooking up?"

"None of your business, Tim," said Zack. "You need to go away. You and your dad have caused us, especially Jenny, enough problems with the way you're stalking us."

"Hey, I don't know what you're talking about," Tim replied. He made his voice sound innocent, but when he looked at the three of them, he wiggled his eyebrows. Jenny was furious and determined that he wouldn't find out anything.

"Hey, Tim," Jenny said. "You might want to let your dad know that the little box I found yesterday had some interesting things in it."

"What do you mean?" asked Tim. "What did you find? He didn't tell me about that."

"You need to ask him. And you need to tell him to leave me alone. I've hidden the box in a safe place, and he had better not try to steal it from me."

"Hey, my dad isn't a thief!" At that, Tim stalked off.

"What are you talking about Jenny? What box?" asked Zack.

Jenny sighed. "We had so much to talk about with the baseball diamond that I didn't even get to tell you about my day yesterday. I'll show you the box later when Tim is nowhere around." She brought Zack and Kate up to speed with the story of finding the box followed by the chase down the mountain. "Mr. Grimes scared me to death. I don't know what he would have done to me if he'd caught me! But the biggest surprise of all is that Whiskers is really just a nice old man. He's a homeless Vietnam veteran who lives in different places at the park and out in the country. But he does pay for his food and supplies from the small diamonds he's able to mine at the crater." She chose not to share that he was currently living at the Mauney House.

Kate's mouth had dropped open. "I can't believe all of that happened to you yesterday, Jenny! Why in the world did you tell Tim the box had something valuable when it doesn't?"

"I figure we can get out to the ball field. Maybe Tim will tell his dad about the box, and they'll go on a wild goose chase out to our RV. *That* will keep them out of our hair."

22

"You know, you kids may be onto something," said Grandma Jo. Even though they wanted nothing more than to get to the ball field, Grandma Jo had insisted they sit down and have a quick snack first. "I know you are all hungry, and I've already put a frozen pizza in the oven. You like Canadian bacon, right, Jenny?" Jenny gave an eager nod. Someone finally knew her favorite! "We can talk and eat at the same time."

Being careful not to burn their mouths in their rush, the trio ate the pizza while Grandma Jo mused. "That ball field has been out there where the prisoner of war camp was located ever since I was a girl. Maybe Hans did hide the diamond out there. Let me get the paper with the list of clues on it." She stood to go retrieve the paper, but before she could take two steps, Kate, Jenny, and Zack started chanting.

"Diamond, ground, corner, base, tree, diamond, diamond, ground, corner, base, tree—"

"Okay, okay, that's enough! I see we don't need to get the list! So are you all finished eating? We need to get our spade and digging tools and get to the ball field. It will be light for just another hour."

Grandma Jo continued, "Zack, I'll give your mother a quick call and let her know that I'll be happy to take you home later, so she won't worry. Jenny, we'll go by the mill and put a note on your dad's truck so he'll know where to find us when he gets off work." She paused, looking at the wide-eyed children. "Come on, let's go! Do you think you're the only ones who want to find this diamond? I grew up hearing about it at least once or twice a month. If it is possible that you've figured out the clues, then I'm in! I want to be there when it is found!"

Shocked into silence at Grandma Jo's enthusiasm, Jenny, Kate, and Zack helped her gather what she thought they'd need, and they loaded into the car. Within a few minutes, they were at the ball field.

Getting out of the car, the kids started to run to the field. Fortunately, no one else was nearby. "Wait," called Grandma Jo. "Let's think this through a little bit. Where do you think we should start?"

"While I was thinking about it during school, I figured Hans had hidden it underneath one of the bases. That would be at a corner, underground. I imagined we'd just have to find the base that had a tree near it. But"—Jenny looked around—"none of these bases really have a tree near them." She sighed heavily. "Don't tell me we are going to have to dig on all four corners of something again!"

"No, Jenny," said Kate. "No we won't! Look over there." Kate took off running. Zack gave a shrug and took off as well. Jenny followed.

"See, it's a tree stump! When my dad was still alive, this is where I used to sit and watch him when he played softball with his work's baseball league. I would sit here and watch him play his position at third base. You can tell by these faded rings in the tree stump that this was once a huge tree. I remember Dad telling me that lightning struck it, and that's why it was cut down."

Approaching the children, Grandma Jo beamed at Kate. "We won't know unless we dig. Here kids, take these spades and shovels and get after it!"

With an energy that surprised them, they attacked third base. After about thirty minutes, Jenny's shovel hit something. "Wait!" she said. "There's something down here!"

All four of them gathered closer. The sun was starting to drop in the sky, but they still had enough light to see by. "Grandma Jo, can you hand me that little gardening trowel?" Jenny asked.

Grandma Jo handed it to her. "Go slowly, Jenny, we don't know how Hans might have wrapped or hidden the diamond if he did bury it here."

Jenny concentrated. Biting her lip, she held the trowel and carefully scraped the layers of dirt away. It appeared that she'd uncovered a leather bag of some sort. Prying carefully with her fingers, she finally got a corner to lift from the soil. "Zack, I can't seem to get this out, can you help?" she asked.

Zack tugged, and then Kate gave it a try. "I think it's starting to come up. Oh, Grandma Jo, I'm so excited!" They exchanged looks as Kate lifted the oil-stained leather pouch from the soil.

Kate handed it to Jenny. "Here," she said. "I think you should be the one to see what is inside. You're the one who had the determination to keep searching and not give up."

Jenny looked at the pouch in her hand. After the disappointment of the metal box, she was almost afraid to open it.

"Hey! What are you guys up to?"

Jenny looked up. "Dad!" she cried excitedly. "Mrs. Lancaster read a story today in class, and then the whole list of Hans' clues finally made sense, and we just had to come out here, and we found this and—"

"Whoa," said Dad. "I think I get the picture." He grinned at Grandma Jo. "Open it, Jenny, and then you can tell me the rest of the story."

Very carefully, Jenny loosened the pouch's drawstring.

"Be careful, Jenny, if it is the diamond it will be small, and we don't want to lose it!"

Jenny nodded her understanding. Stretching the top of the pouch, it opened easily once she gently loosened the leather string. If it had been buried by Hans, it would have been hidden away for over sixty years.

"Just think," said Kate, "if this is the diamond, then Hans would have actually held that pouch in his hand. He would have been the last person to touch it!"

Holding out her left hand, Jenny lifted the pouch in her right and started to gently shake it. At first nothing happened, then a flash of glitter caught the late afternoon sun.

"It's here!" cried Jenny. "It's the German diamond! But wait . . ." She paused. "I think there's something else!"

She handed the pouch to Grandma Jo, who continued to gently shake it. Not just one diamond, but four others tumbled out. The large stones would make several large cut diamonds for jewelry. "It looks like Hans took more than he wrote about," she said wryly.

Twisting her head around to look at Dad, Jenny asked the question that had been burning in her heart for weeks. "Can we stay now, Dad?"

Dad gave his head a nod. "You always were a persistent one! Yes, Jenny, it looks like we'll be able to stay."

—⚬⚬⚬—

Later That Fall

"I don't know when I haven't been the one cooking the Thanksgiving turkey. It feels strange!"

"It's, okay, Grandma Jo," said Kate. "I'm sure Jenny's dad knows how to roast a turkey."

"I can't wait to visit them in their house! Jenny thought she wouldn't be here once the weather turned cold, and now they are regular residents in town."

The pair strolled down the walk leading to the Garrison house. The shrubs had been trimmed, and there were two fat orange pumpkins sitting on either side of the front porch steps. Giving the front door a knock, Kate and Grandma Jo waited.

"Come on in!" said Jenny as she swung the door open wide. "The turkey will be ready soon."

"Welcome," called Dad. "We are glad you could join us for our first Thanksgiving in our home!"

Their table was set for seven. Jenny and her dad had been able to rent the house and then had gone shopping at the secondhand store and found the table and a few other pieces of furniture they needed. In the RV, all the furniture had been attached, and there was no way they could move it into the house to use.

Looking up, Kate saw Whiskers come out of the kitchen. "Hi," she said shyly. "My name is Kate."

"Hi, Kate," he said. "My name is Carl. I want you to know that I'm so happy for you kids finding the diamonds. And I'm sorry I scared you all so much that day in the park. I was just worried about your safety."

"I understand. Jenny told me why you did it, and I appreciate you looking out for us." Kate turned to Jenny. "Who else is coming for dinner?"

"Zack and his mom," replied Jenny. "We decided it would be wonderful to celebrate with everyone who befriended us when we first moved here."

"All's well that ends well," said Grandma Jo. "I was pleased with what the jeweler up in Fayetteville paid you for the stones. All three of you kids have your college fund now and will be able to go to school wherever you want.

And Grimes will have to spend a little time in county jail for his charges of breaking and entering. I'll never figure out where he got the fool idea of breaking into your RV. I don't mean to be rude, but why would he think there was something valuable there?"

Jenny and Kate smiled and exchanged a look.

"But the best part of all, Jenny," continued Grandma Jo, "is that you and your dad got to finally move into a house. We're real glad that you are here to stay."

There was another knock on the door. "That must be Zack and his mom. Coming!" Jenny hollered at the door. She turned back to Grandma Jo. "I'm glad, too. We've finally come home."

Acknowledgments

Research is an important part of my books. I want to thank Waymon Cox, Crater of Diamonds State Park interpreter, for valuable insight and information about the park during my research trip. I also need to give special thanks to my family of readers who read the manuscript and gave feedback. Venda, Summer, Jacqueline, Lauretta, and Becca, your comments were invaluable.

About the Author

Brenda Turner is a National Board Certified Teacher and a facilitator for gifted and talented students. She is a public speaker and writes and publishes classroom curriculum materials. Her first book was *Cimarron Sunrise*. Brenda has two adult daughters and lives in Northwest Arkansas with her husband.

Contact Brenda at
brendaturnerbooks.com.